I0542044

Starting Over

THE OTHER MAN

MATTHEW J. METZGER

The Other Man
ISBN # 978-1-83943-808-0
©Copyright Matthew J. Metzger 2019
Cover Art by Erin Dameron-Hill ©Copyright October 2019
Interior text design by Claire Siemaszkiewicz
Pride Publishing

THE OTHER MAN

Dedication

Of course, this one's for Matti.

Chapter One

Gabriel didn't stir when Aled removed the collar.

He was a mess. A ridiculously beautiful, tempting mess. The collar had left a thin red line on his alabaster skin, framed by the bruises either side where Aled had bitten him. His legs were in a similar state, especially his inner thighs. Aled liked Gabriel's inner thighs, and it showed. One wrist was a little swollen from all the twisting around he'd done on their first day, and Aled made a mental note to check it again once they were home.

He ghosted his fingers over the raised skin and squeezed.

Nothing.

"Unbelievable," he muttered and shook Gabriel by the shoulder. "Come on, Gabe. We need to go."

Gabriel hated that nickname. Usually it earned Aled the mother of all scowls. But this time? Nothing.

"*Gabe.*"

A low grumble emanated from the inert lump, and it became even more lumplike — the hand in Aled's slid free, seized the duvet and pulled. In a heartbeat, Gabriel was buried in the rumpled remains of the bed and not an inch of skin could be seen.

"I guess age really is just a number."

Aled wanted to leave him to it, but it was quarter to eleven and they only had fifteen minutes to check out and return the keys. And *he* was ready to go. Their bags were by the door, tidily packed. Every surface was clean. He'd even done the last sweep of the bathroom to check for abandoned soap or forgotten aftershave. The only thing left was to pour Gabriel into a T-shirt and jeans and stuff him in the car.

Which—from a lot of experience—Aled knew was easier said than done.

It wasn't that difficult if Gabriel was just asleep. Turfing him out of bed for work in the morning was easy enough. But after a game? No chance. And it had been a *long* game.

They'd met nearly two years ago after a random hook-up on Grindr. Aled had been going through a divorce, and Gabriel had been—still was—a sex fiend. They'd figured out pretty fast that Aled's dominant tendencies and Gabriel's sexual fantasies lined up neatly, and had been playing on a regular basis ever since. Hence the collar.

And hence the coma, because Gabriel after a whole weekend of being used and abused could sleep like the dead.

"All right," Aled said, turning up the bottom of the duvet. "You leave me no choice."

He found an ankle. The minute he wrapped his fingers around it, the leg was dragged away. But Aled was used to pinning down fighting bodies and simply pitted his weight against Gabriel's. And given Gabriel was a wiry little wretch and Aled was in his mid-thirties and growing an appropriately sized spare tyre around his gut, it was always going to go in his favour.

Dragging on the ankle produced a calf. At the other end of the calf lay the sensitive back of a knee. And above that, a thigh that Aled could seize in both hands and use like a lever. A moment later, he had an armful of squirming plaything, and he squeezed Gabriel to his chest in a bear hug before standing up and depositing that battered, naked body on the rug.

Then dark eyes were staring up at him from the vicinity of his crotch, and his brain short-circuited.

Maybe they could be a *little* la —

He shook himself. No. The cabin had been expensive enough. Paying for a whole extra day wasn't on the cards.

"If you're in that car in the next five minutes, I'll fuck you at the border," he offered.

"You won't."

Gabriel's voice was raspy and hoarse. He'd spent the better part of seventy-two hours either screaming, begging or gagged. His lips were still flushed and swollen and the breathy quality to his words was another unhelpful aphrodisiac.

Aled raised his eyebrows and straightened his spine. That cool edge of power started to flicker around the edges of his psyche once more.

"I will."

"You're chafing."

Aled winced. He *was* a bit raw. "Don't need my cock to count as a fuck."

"No deal."

He laughed, the mood dissipating. He knew that tone.

"All right, beautiful. But we do need to go. I'll buy you lunch at the border, how's that?"

That was apparently more agreeable. Gabriel pushed himself up on shaky limbs and reached for the clothes Aled had laid out.

Gabriel's twenty-sixth birthday had been at the weekend and Aled's present had been a long, *long* sex game. They were both kinky, despite Aled's bland ginger-with-glasses, chubby-thirties and job-in-marketing appearance. Aled wasn't always entirely *comfortable* with his sexual preferences — who got off on rape fantasies, after all? — but Gabriel had no such room for doubts. He liked nothing more than to be dragged down fighting and fucked raw.

So that was what Aled had done. From Friday afternoon right through to Monday morning.

He'd 'kidnapped' Gabriel from work and driven him up to this lonely, snow-covered cabin in the Scottish Highlands. It was intended for hikers, but they'd never left. In the midst of a dark forest, miles from civilisation and buried under three and a half feet of snow, he had treated Gabriel like a sex slave — and there hadn't been a whisper of a safeword the entire time.

Basically, he'd fucked Gabriel stupid for his birthday.

"Come on," he coaxed, when he'd come back from putting the bags in the car and found Gabriel still shirtless. "We need to go."

"Don't want to go."

Aled laughed. "You sound like a petulant kid."

"I'm on holiday!"

"We have to check out at eleven. Tell you what," Aled added when Gabriel scowled. "We'll stop for a massive pub lunch at the border, and I'll blow you in the toilets after if you're good and don't flirt with half the country on the way down."

Gabriel grumbled but tilted his head back against Aled's shoulder. Aled obediently kissed his ear.

That had been the basis of the game. They had an open relationship by mutual agreement—Gabriel regularly slept with other men, and had full-blown relationships with at least one of them. Aled had the same option in theory, but so far hadn't indulged. It worked, and worked well. But some of Aled's favourite games were when he pretended it was a problem. So, the kidnap had been on the premise that he was sick of Gabriel's playing away. He'd spent the weekend reminding Gabriel who he belonged to.

Supposedly. The truth was somewhere in the middle. Aled *didn't* mind the playing away. He even liked it sometimes, for the way he could exploit it for their own games—and not having to do bloodplay. But—

Lately, he'd found himself getting tired of driving Gabriel home after their scenes. Of booking taxis to and from the flat and the house. Of having to make sure they left enough time at the end of an evening to go their separate ways.

Aled didn't *want* to go their separate ways anymore.

But Gabriel was still a wild thing. Completely undomesticated. Aled was sure he'd baulk at the idea of living together and run a mile. So Aled hadn't said anything. What they had was great. Why risk it for the sake of an extra cuddle in the morning? So Aled kissed Gabriel's ear again and let go, smacking his arse to propel him towards the door. He wanted more—but it wasn't worth risking everything over.

"Can I have my phone back?" Gabriel asked as he wriggled into a bra and T-shirt, inky black hair sticking up all over the place in an impressive bedhead.

Aled raised an eyebrow sardonically. "Excuse me?"

Gabriel paused then dropped his gaze. "Please can I have my phone back, sir?"

"Why."

It wasn't a question — it was a demand.

"To — to check my messages, sir — "

"Has someone been messaging you?"

"I don't know."

"I haven't been messaging you. Who else could be?"

"Nobody important, sir."

"Damn right," Aled drawled. "And if it's nobody important, then you don't need to see it. Do you?"

"No, sir."

"Then I think I'll keep hold of it a while longer."

Gabriel swallowed, but nodded. "Yes, sir."

"Go out to the car, then. And no more arguing."

He was too raw for another fuck, or even a blow job. But after the hint of more playing, his libido was interested again. So once he'd locked up, he turned on Gabriel at the car and shoved him up against the boot, pressing his chest into the cold glass of the rear windscreen.

"Drop 'em and bend over."

"Sir?"

"*Now.*"

Gabriel fumbled with his jeans. "Please don't," he said and Aled heard the veiled warning. "It'll hurt — "

"I'm not going to fuck you," he said calmly, drawing the toy from his coat pocket. "I'd fall asleep at the wheel. But you obviously need a bit more practice with your lessons."

The plug was small, Aled's concession to Gabriel's soreness, but he pushed it in relentlessly and dry, forcing Gabriel still with a hand on his hip, until it was buried to the base. Gabriel whined, and Aled kissed his neck as he pulled the jeans back up and zipped Gabriel back in.

"Get fussy on the way home, and I'll switch it on."

Gabriel shuddered, and Aled backed up. He slapped his arse again, hard, and Gabriel near-yowled.

"Get in the car. Your phone's in the glovebox. On flight mode. You keep it that way — you can play your stupid games, but you don't put it on the network and start playing away again, got it?"

"Yes, sir."

Aled turned him, fisted a hand in Gabriel's hair and kissed him properly. He could still taste sex and salt on Gabriel's tongue. It was a heady combination, but it was also too soon for anything more.

Aled drew off and shoved. "Go."

Gabriel went.

* * * *

They stopped near the English–Scottish border for lunch. Gabriel had fallen asleep and Aled woke him up by finding the remote for the plug and switching it on, to earn himself a yelp, a sour look and a question about the validity of his parents' marriage.

"Afternoon to you too, sweetheart." He laughed and leaned over to kiss Gabriel's jaw.

Gabriel blinked. "Game over?"

"Unless you want to continue?"

Gabriel chewed on his lip then cocked his head. "No—but I still want you to take your plug back when we get home."

"Deal," Aled said, grinning. "Come on. I need feeding. You don't get to keep belly rolls like this without pub lunches."

"Oh right, yeah, you're a *real* fatso," Gabriel said mockingly.

He was bright and bubbly, chatting up a barmaid — much to Aled's amusement—and grilling Aled on whether he liked her.

"She's not bad," Aled said. "Bit young for me, though."

"She's twenty!"

"And I'm thirty-five in the New Year. She was in nappies when I was finding out what girls were all about. Too young."

Gabriel cackled. "When *I* was figuring out boys, *you* were getting married."

"You would have been around fourteen when I got married."

"Yeah, figuring out boys."

"I refuse to believe you reached fourteen before you were shagging other boys," Aled said flatly.

"Good call, but I was fourteen before I was any good at it."

Gabriel's phone beeped on the table, the text message icon flashing up. Aled's hand shot out, quick as lightning, and he had it in his palm before Gabriel could even put down his burger long enough to pick it up.

"Hey!"

"This isn't flight mode."

Gabriel smirked. "You said game over."

"Might change my mind."

"Don't."

Aled raised his eyebrows. "Colour?"

They had a system. Aled's only serious relationship before Gabriel had been very simple. The safeword was no. End of story. But Gabriel liked to say no when he meant yes, so had brought a traffic light system to the table. Red was easy. Green was easy.

Gabriel hesitated then shook his head. "Yellow, I guess?"

And yellow was somewhere in the middle.

"You guess? Gabe—"

"—riel!"

Aled smirked and rolled his eyes.

"I'm interested, but I'm sore," Gabriel said, chewing on his lip as though mentally chewing on his words. "And I thought I'd feel *less* sore after my nap, but I don't. I need a long soak in a hot bath before you do anything else or it'll really hurt, and not in a good way."

Aled nodded, turning the phone over in his free hand. "All right. Rain check. To be honest, I wouldn't be fucking you anyway. My dick's just about ready to crawl up into my body and hibernate."

"Old man."

"Oi! Who's too sore for a beating here?"

Gabriel actually stuck out his tongue, so Aled responded by being equally childish and throwing a chip at him. Gabriel snatched it up and ate it, grinning.

"Twat," Aled said affectionately, thumbing open the text. "It's from Michael."

"Surprise, surprise."

"Why the sarcasm?"

"You beat him to the punch. He wanted to take me for some city break on the continent for my birthday. *And* Christmas."

Michael was one of Gabriel's other regulars — in fact, since some lad called Justin had gone serious with a Huddersfield bloke, Michael and Kevin were the only other regulars left. Kevin was even kinkier than Aled. Michael, as far as Aled could gather, was more vanilla.

"Bit romantic, isn't it?"

"Not really. You don't start a romantic city break with an offer to fuck in the train toilets."

"Grim," Aled opined, glancing over the text.

Then frowned. There were a few of them.

Michael: Hey angel when you back? Missing the sight of your pretty arse on the end of my dick.

Michael: Woke up with wood this morning. Need an angel to come take care of it.

Michael: You back by Wednesday? Got the day off work, could come round and give you something to do.

Something flickered in Aled's gut.

Something hot and angry. Something bad. Something unfamiliar that soured his mood and made him click back out of the texts and pocket the phone.

Something *jealous*.

Chapter Two

Gabriel sank down in the bath until even his lips were below the surface, and sighed.

Good, that felt good.

He'd initially wanted to go home and have some space, but then Aled had offered a hot bath for his aches and pains and the house all to himself.

"Suze wants me to go round for a couple of drinks with her," he'd said. "Make yourself at home. If you want to go back to the flat later, there'll be some emergency notes in the top kitchen drawer, so use those."

Gabriel wiggled his toes in the hot water and thought it over.

Part of him wanted to go home. His own bed, his own space, just spread out in the sheets and catch up on his messages. And part of him wanted to stay the night. His flat didn't have a bath. And — though he'd never tell Aled, because that would be confessing that Aled had won him over to the octopus routine — he quite fancied being woken up by some soft, sleepy snuggling in the morning.

That was the biggest danger with Aled. Not the sex games going too far, or that scary cage in the garage for when Gabriel was *seriously* out of line, or even Aled's thing for knives that Gabriel had so far refused to indulge. It was being cooked to death by a cuddle in his sleep. The man was like a clingy, overheated beanbag.

And Gabriel wouldn't admit it even under threat of the most savage beating Kevin could give him, but…he liked the idea of a bit of snuggling tonight.

He surfaced a little, tipping his head back to submerge his hair and ears.

"Happy birthday to me," he murmured.

Fucked dumb, then a hot bath and a long cuddle? It didn't get better than that.

His phone beeped on the side of the bath, and Gabriel opened a single eye, considering it. It could be Aled. He was really good about the alcohol. If he was drunk, he'd stay the night with Suze. And if he wasn't, then he'd bring back food.

Food.

Gabriel could go for a massive cheese pizza.

He wiped a hand off on the towel draped over the sink and reached for the phone. Two messages. And neither from Aled. He mulled it over then swiped into them. At least Kevin would need answering.

Kevin: You back from Scotland?

Me: Yep :) Soaking in the bath.

He swiped out and went for the other one, but Kevin was clearly waiting up for an answer, and a reply was pinged back in seconds.

Kevin: Everything okay?

Me: Fanfuckingtastic :D

Kevin: Take it he fucked you a new hole?

Me: I think my ovaries fell out at some point. He was nearly as savage as you ;)

Kevin: Nobody's as savage as me ;)

Me: Not legally anyway.

Kevin: Point. Have a good birthday then?

Me: The best :) I'll come round and visit you and Judith soon. I wanna see the new baby! Is there a name yet?

Kevin was family. He and Gabriel had met in the same way he'd met Aled — Grindr, a one-night stand and a discovery of mutual kinks that made regular fucking a good idea. But just like Aled, Kevin had turned into something more.

But different.

Gabriel loved them both — but Kevin was like a close friend, a confidant, a mentor, a support system. Aled was a lover. And that was the difference. Gabriel never wanted to *be* with Kevin. He didn't want silly dates with Kevin. He wouldn't go and visit Kevin's nan. Kevin was — a friend. An exceptionally close one, and with considerable sexual benefits, but a friend all the same.

A friend who'd saved Gabriel's life, in more ways than one.

He'd helped Gabriel beat the alcoholism. He'd kept him sober in the darkest moments. He'd seen him at his absolute worst and still sat with him, still helped him, still wanted him. Still *cared*. And while Gabriel at twenty-six could point to many people who cared, he'd not been able to do the same at twenty.

And because Kevin *had* seen him at his worst—and had been largely responsible for getting him out of it again—he was the only one allowed to instigate rules outside of games. Gabriel was a sexual submissive, but he *hated* lifestyle submission. Aled could order him around all he wanted when they were having sex, but like hell Gabriel was going to be listening if Aled tried any of that shit when they were out for a walk or planning a trip to the beach or whatever.

But Kevin?

Kevin was the exception.

And the big, inviolable rule was *stay in touch*.

Whatever Gabriel did, wherever he was, he had to stay in touch. At least once a week, he had to let Kevin know he was all right. Even if it was just a stupid selfie, or a smiley face—it had to be *something*.

Kevin: We think we've finally agreed on one. Apparently Kevinella is still not allowed :(

Me: That's a horrible name. Judith should name all your children.

Kevin: Oh sure, take her side.

Me: Us subs have to stick together :)

Kevin: I'm going to remember that next time you come round here begging for a beating.

Me: Ummm…

Kevin: You free next weekend?

Me: I'm washing my arse-hair.

Kevin: For dinner, you tart. Come round for dinner and see the brats. I can inspect you after ;)

Me: I know how you like to inspect people, no thanks ;) Saturday? I might be working Sunday.

If he still had a job. Rumours were swirling that they were going to close the shop, but Gabriel was too content to care. Let them. It was a shit job anyway.

Kevin: Saturday it is. Say hi to Aled for us, and he's welcome too if he wants. Happy birthday x

Gabriel smirked. Aled wouldn't want. He *hated* kids. He didn't even come in the house to pick Gabriel up if he suspected the kids might be home.

Contact duty done, he swiped out of Kevin's messages and opened the other one – and immediately rolled his eyes.

Michael: I have a problem.

"Let me guess," Gabriel muttered to himself. "It's ten inches long and fits perfectly inside me." He sent a single question mark and waited.

Michael: It's ten inches long and fits perfectly inside you ;)

"Oh, hey, I'm psychic."

Michael: Missed you ;)

Michael: You home?

Me: Nope, staying the night.

Michael: He must have a good meat stick!!

Gabriel mimed vomiting. Until Michael, he'd never met anyone who actually *said* that. Michael had even referred to his cunt as an oven mitten once. The guy was seriously weird.

Michael: Sack him off and I'll come round ;) I could hammer nails with this but I'd rather hammer you xxx

Me: Can't, sorry :) And I'm back at work next week so I need my beauty sleep.

Michael: You're beautiful anyway.

Gabriel softened. That was ni —

Michael: And spunk is good for the skin ;)

"Or maybe not."

Michael: Wanna sext?

Then there was a dick pic. Michael was having one off the wrist. Gabriel tilted the picture and squinted, then laughed.

Me: Who jacks off to the news?

Michael: New sports commentator ;) Not as good as you, though. Cock is all ready for you. Come over and it'll wear you like a glove xxx

Me: Not right now it won't. I'm all fucked out.

Michael: You'll be fine ;) I'll go gentle. Come over x

Gabriel rolled his eyes. Michael was a good lay for one reason and one reason only — it hit all of Gabriel's dirty sex-toy kinks. Because that was all he felt like when Michael fucked him. He was a hole for Michael to stick his dick into — and that was all that ever happened. He rammed that pole of his inside — and whatever Michael said, it was seven inches, not ten — pumped twice and it was all over. He'd pull out, tuck himself in and that was that.

Gabriel was nothing more than a living fleshlight.

And when he was in the mood for that, it was great. Seedy and filthy and anonymous, without the danger of *actual* anonymous where guys could wig out at being presented with so-called lady bits instead of what they'd been expecting. When he wanted to feel like a cheap whore but didn't want an involved game, Michael was the perfect screw.

In every other aspect, he was crap.

He didn't know how to work Gabriel's gear. He either didn't know or didn't care about preparation. And he lasted about a minute. It was hardly worth the bother of going round to Michael's flat in the first place.

Submerged in the bath, surrounded by the sauna of Aled's bathroom, and with a phone full of friendly flirting and not-so-suitable welfare checks from his closest friend, Gabriel didn't particularly want to feel like a whore. He didn't want any sex at all right that second, but if he *had* to, he'd take Kevin's predatory filming, or Aled's tongue-fucking to convince him he liked it. Time. Effort. Expertise. The sense that it was about *him*, that it had to be *him*, even if he was supposedly being forced or coerced.

Not—Michael.

Me: Sorry.

He wasn't.

Me: Sometime soon :)

Maybe.

Chapter Three

Aled kept a lid on it.

He took Gabriel back to the house. Made dinner. Ran a bath when Gabriel asked him to check why his arse hurt so much and dropped his jeans to reveal a burst and bleeding welt. Treated it with the first-aid kit and snuck in a couple of apology kisses to the rest of the affected cheek. Then left Gabriel to soak and replied to Suze's begging texts for some company.

And only when he'd buckled himself back into the car did he allow the jealousy — and the corresponding confusion — to take over.

He'd never been a jealous man. He simply wasn't. He'd been one hundred percent happy for Suze when she'd gone gaga for Tom in university. He'd kissed his then-wife at the door and told her to be safe when she'd gone out on the pull with her girlfriends. He'd sorted their respective porn collections to minimise accidental crossover without a murmur. He'd known from the very first time he'd slept with Gabriel that he wasn't the only one doing it. So what? He'd never *cared*.

So why had those texts from Michael made him feel sick? Why had he had the urge to delete them, delete *him* and rub him out of Gabriel's life?

God, it was pathetic. And it was a problem.

Aled freely admitted he wasn't especially wired to be polygamous himself — he'd slept with maybe five other people in his open marriage, and nobody at all since meeting Gabriel — but he'd never placed any demand for exclusivity on either his ex-wife or his current partner. But how could he not, if he was starting to get jealous? And what did that mean for *them*, when Gabriel had always been so forthright and honest about his own preferences?

Gabriel would not — possibly *could* not — narrow down his sex and love life to Aled alone.

A crack formed in the middle of Aled's chest, aching and sore, as he wondered what he was supposed to do about this. And how he was supposed to do it. Gabriel might love him and trust him, but he was still a naturally wary sort of person. Aled still had to tread carefully with important discussions — and he'd *intended* to have one when they were away.

And had chickened out.

As usual.

Which was why when Suze had texted asking if he was free, he'd said yes.

Suze could keep a secret. Suze would help. Suze had helped him come to terms with his aggressive tastes in sex. Suze had helped him come to terms with his divorce. And Suze could help him with this.

So he left Gabriel soaking in the bath, and went straight round.

Suze and Tom had moved to Wrenthorpe in the summer. Privately, Aled thought the house was hideous. A squat redbrick with enormous windows like bulging eyes and a violently ugly porch jutting out in front like a squashed beak. It was revolting. But Suze called it cute, and Tom had fallen in love with the view over some fields to the back, and that was that. And Aled did have to admit it was nice being able to use a driveway instead of leaving the car in the road at the mercy of all the boy racers round where they used to live.

Suze had wet, freshly dyed hair when she answered the door, dressed in a pair of bunny slippers, her tartan pyjama bottoms and nothing else. Aled just pulled a face at her tits and asked if she wanted him to go to the Chinese at the end of the road and get their usual.

"Way ahead of you," she said. "There's pizza in the oven and wine in the fridge. Where's my hug, you slag?"

Suze had been Aled's best friend since school. *Infant* school. They'd grown up together, gone to the same university, shared a flat in second year together and — albeit by coincidence — even ended up working for the same company. Suze had been Aled's best man at his wedding, and she was threatening him with a bridesmaid's dress if she ever married Tom. They'd fought, rowed, sulked, not spoken, even outright feuded — and yet they always came back together again. She could slap some sense into him or let him cry on her shoulder. Aled was an only child, but he had the feeling that he knew what it was like to have a sister.

And with the confusion and anxiety smashing up against each other in his head about this newfound jealousy, he needed his sister.

So he reached, and squeezed her tight in a hug until she squeaked.

"Oh," she said. "What's up?"

He grumbled into her shoulder.

"Oh my God, did you ask Gabriel to—"

"Chickened out," he admitted.

"Aled! Why?"

"I don't know, the fear he'd dump me for being too clingy?"

"It's been two years! Asking him to move in with you isn't clingy!" she chided. "It's weird you've waited this long!"

"Because I don't want him to think it's getting too—serious."

"Too serious? You are dating. For two years. You are stupidly in love with him and you have keys to his flat. How is this *not* serious?"

Aled locked the front door, leaned against it and blurted out, "I'm fucked."

"Sorry?"

"I'm fucked," he repeated, and ran both hands through his hair. "One of his other regulars texted him while we were away. Asking when he'd be back and offering a fuck and the usual. And I got *jealous*, Suze."

Suze paused.

She simply stood in the hall, a topless drowned rat, and stared.

Then she said, "Oh."

"Yeah," Aled said weakly.

"Right."

"Yeah."

"Right. Kitchen. Now."

Aled nodded and went into the kitchen. Suze vanished upstairs. He poured out some wine and—screw measures—filled the glasses until they threatened to brim over, then took up a spot at the breakfast bar. He drained a glass then refilled it and nursed the second one properly. He chewed on his thoughts until Suze reappeared, now clad in a dressing gown, and threw another at him. The spare. *His* spare. It had lived in Suze's various flats and houses ever since they'd stopped living together after their second year at university, for moments just like this.

Aled shrugged it on over his T-shirt and jeans and buried his nose in the warm collar.

"Right," Suze said, taking her wine glass. "Talk to me. You got jealous of one of his other regular guys?"

"Yeah."

"Jealous like…how?"

"Like I wanted to punch the guy."

"For what?"

"For — for saying he wanted Gabriel to come back to Leeds soon so they could fuck. It wasn't even particularly raunchy stuff."

"Is this the other kinky guy, or — "

"No, the vanilla one. Michael."

"The weightlifter?"

"No, that one's got a boyfriend now."

"Right," Suze said again then winced. "So what are you going to do?"

"I've got no idea," Aled confessed.

"Do you think maybe it's a one-time thing, or — "

"I hope so, but what if it's not?"

Suze bit her lip. "Well, you'll need to talk about it."

"Talk to Gabriel about it? Are you kidding? He'll freak and run a mile. He doesn't do jealous doms."

"If you don't, he'll pick up on something being wrong anyway, and God knows what he'll think has fucked you off."

Aled winced.

"You will need to talk to him."

"Yeah — "

Suze cocked her head, frowning. "This isn't like you. You never got jealous of Melissa's other regular guys.

And I thought you had dinner with that kinky guy Gabriel likes? Kieran?"

"Kevin. I did. He's nice. He did your kitchen refit, remember?"

"Oh, *that* guy?" For a moment, she grinned. "Gabriel has good taste."

Aled rolled his eyes.

"So where's this come from, then? What did the texts *say*?"

"They were just—crass. You know, shit like, 'when are you back, I have something for you to do' and 'I miss seeing your arse around my cock.' Just crass Grindr-type shit."

"What if he'd said—I don't know, 'I miss you' or just 'when are you home, we could get together next week if you're free?'"

Aled hesitated. "I—I don't think I'd have minded that so much."

"So, it's this guy being all crass and overly sexual that bothered you?"

"Maybe."

"Or maybe it's the lack of care?"

Aled blinked. "Sorry?"

"Well, this other guy, Kieran—"

"Kevin."

" —what if he'd texted saying 'get your arse over here' or sent a dick pic or something?"

Nothing happened. No flare of anger. No twitch in his brain. Nothing.

"That—doesn't bother me."

"But you know Kevin cares, don't you?" Suze pressed. "You've met him once or twice. You know he takes care of Gabriel as much as you do."

"I—yeah."

Kevin did extreme stuff. Stuff even Aled thought was too far. Gabriel always came back from shagging Kevin looking like he'd gone ten rounds with a professional boxer. But Kevin was also Gabriel's best friend, and if he came back smashed up, he also came bright and buoyant and brimming over with energy. He came back beautiful.

"Does Michael?"

"Does he what?"

"Care."

"I don't know."

"Well, if he did, would that make it better?" Suze asked. "Like, if he's all crass and let's fuck and rude by text but in person, he's—I don't know, he likes to cuddle, and he picks Gabriel up from work when it's raining, all that nice person stuff?"

"I don't *know*, Suze," Aled said in frustration. "I can theorise but I don't *know*. What if this guy hacks me off just by being around? What if—"

What if it wasn't just him?

What if it was just Michael right now, but it would be the next guy too? And Kevin? And *anyone* else? And—

Gabriel would walk.

"Stop it," Suze said. "Stop panicking and just think, okay?"

Aled swallowed.

"Michael might be fine. You might like him. If this issue is that you think he doesn't care, then all you have to do is get some evidence that he does. Maybe meet him, maybe see more of his text messages, talk to Gabriel about what he's like. I mean, Michael could look at you just the same."

Aled frowned. "How do you mean?"

"Well, some of what you text each other probably looks really awful if you don't know about BDSM and stuff."

Aled paused. That was true. But—

"Michael's vanilla."

"Even vanilla people like porn and dirty talk sometimes. Tom's so vanilla he's practically just milk, but even he likes to call me a slut occasionally when I'm sucking him off."

Aled grimaced. "Really? *Tom*?"

"It's the closest he gets to being good in bed," she said dismissively, then waved a hand. "Back to the point. Maybe Michael's fine and you just caught something out of context. I think you need a bigger picture before you go jumping to some conclusion that you're a madly jealous shit and there's going to be major problems."

Aled groaned, rubbing the back of his neck. She was talking sense, but—

"And what if I am? What if Michael's a complete cunt and I'm jealous of him? What if he's *not* a shit and I'm *still* jealous of him?"

"Then I guess you and Gabriel need to talk about how to handle that. Maybe Gabriel would be willing to let this one guy go if you're super clear that you're not asking for monogamy. Or maybe Gabriel just not talking about him anymore would solve the issue and you can feign ignorance and feel fine about it."

"I can't ask him to move in now," Aled said desperately. "You know what he's like, if he thinks I'm getting jealous *and* trying to get more control over his life—"

"But you're not."

"—at the same time—he won't see it like that, Suze."

She hummed, twisting her wine glass between her palms. She'd barely touched it. "Yeah. I see what you mean."

"So what the hell do I do? If I ask him to move in then later bring up I'm jealous of one of his other guys, he'll freak. But if I do it the other way around, he might freak just at the jealous thing, and—"

"Okay, in *his* shoes—I think I would be weirded out more by 'move in with me' followed by 'I don't want you seeing this guy.' That—I don't know, that seems more controlling to me. Less coincidental. You know, that's—that's the kind of thing you see building up in those domestic violence storylines on the soaps."

"Shall I pretend I watch the soaps?" Aled asked, raising an eyebrow.

"You know what I mean."

He snorted but nodded.

"So, I think you need to talk about Michael first. And pause the moving-in question until everything settles again after that. I mean, if it turns out you've completely got the wrong end of the stick and you're not a bit jealous when you find out he's really into snuggling and kittens and volunteers to help old ladies cross the road, it might all blow over as a complete nothing and you can ask about living together anyway."

Aled smiled but didn't really feel it. Somehow he couldn't see Michael being into kittens and snuggling. The *off* vibe was just too strong. And he was torn between listening to his instincts and telling his instincts not to be so damn judgemental. It wasn't like Aled's career and hobbies were all that predictable from his sexual preferences either.

"And if it's not, and I can't stand the idea of Gabriel anywhere near this guy?"

"Then—yeah. Keep moving as a separate thing, I think. *Really* separate."

Aled nodded, raking his hands through his hair again. "Fucking hell. When did I get *jealous*, Suze?"

"I don't think you are," she said softly, reaching across the breakfast bar to squeeze his hand. "I think it's something about *this* guy, not guys in general."

"Why? How do you know?"

"Because you never have been before. And you were just as nuts about Melissa as you are about Gabriel. And you said yourself, you don't think Kevin's a problem. So I think something about this one guy has rubbed you the wrong way, and I think maybe it's that crassness. I mean, your whole issue with your sex life has always been that you don't like how your aggression comes across. Your aftercare has always been a good cuddle and—well, *care*. Maybe you think this guy doesn't care, and you're wary about trusting someone you love to him. And I think if you frame it that way, and you let Gabriel prove you wrong—if he can—then it'll be okay. You know Kevin cares. And you know that because you sat down with him and talked."

Aled blinked.

It clicked in his head.

He'd—he'd been jealous then, too. Anger at what he'd thought had happened had morphed into this ugly jealousy whenever Gabriel had mentioned Kevin for a whole week, until Aled had decided that he couldn't just ignore things.

Gabriel had come over the week before Christmas with a black eye that would have put a professional boxer to shame. And Aled had hit the roof. Suddenly, that hot rage in his stomach wasn't as unfamiliar as he'd thought—he'd had it before, that Christmas, with

Gabriel trying to explain that it wasn't what it looked like.

And it had taken sitting down with the owner of the fist that had caused it and talking about what they did together.

He'd seen for himself that Kevin wasn't what he looked like. He was like Aled — someone extremely dominant, even violent, when it came to sex and yet harmless outside of it. He cared for Gabriel, just as much — although differently, perhaps — as Aled did. He did things for Gabriel that were too much for Aled to manage, the kind of BDSM that Aled liked in porn but couldn't act out himself. But it had taken sitting down with Kevin, talking about it, and eventually sitting in on a session and watching the way he cared for Gabriel after the fact for Aled to really believe it.

"Shit," Aled said. "It was — it was the same with Kevin."

"What?"

"I felt like this when I thought Kevin had smacked Gabriel around. Remember? Before Christmas, like you said."

Suze blinked. "*That* was why you wanted to talk to him?"

"Yeah. Gabriel came over with a shiner and blood all down his thighs and I flipped my shit."

"Because of Kevin?"

"Yeah, Gabriel had a bad day and nearly came off the wagon, so he went to Kevin and Kevin beat him for it. It's one of their things. And I — you know. Would you believe it, if someone told you that?"

"Not really."

"Exactly."

"But that's great!"

Aled blinked at the sudden tangent. "Is it?"

"Yes!" Suze gave him a megawatt grin. "You got mad, you got jealous, just like now, because you thought this other guy was abusive or taking advantage. And Gabriel didn't dump you, you worked it all out. Together. So talk to Gabe. Tell him it's like that time. And if Michael's actually a sweetheart like Kevin is, then you've nothing to be jealous of and you can get over yourself."

Aled nodded, and his shoulders finally relaxed. They'd worked through the issue with Kevin. No problem. As long as Michael was just like Kevin, then it would be fine, and Aled could get back on track persuading Gabriel to move in.

And if Michael *was* a crass idiot who only saw Gabriel as a place to stick his dick, then —

Then maybe Aled wouldn't feel so bad about trying to persuade them to part ways after all.

Chapter Four

The first day back at work sucked.

Gabriel stacked shelves in a Tesco Express. He didn't have any qualifications to get a proper job, but he'd been doing it long enough that he was at least a fraction above the minimum wage. Sometimes he helped train the new staff. Sometimes he helped old ladies work the self-service checkout. And sometimes he had sex in the stockroom with one of the cashiers—but Jonathan didn't work Tuesdays and Gabriel's spotty teenager of a manager decided to give him another lecture about ambition.

"I don't have work ambitions," Gabriel said, which only served to piss her off. "I'd like to shag someone from every county in the country, though. Does that count?"

It didn't count.

He texted Kevin as he left. He wasn't allowed to walk home after dark on his own—his flat was in a rough neighbourhood and Gabriel didn't pass consistently enough to rely on it being generally a bad idea to approach unknown men in Belle Isle. Whether it was Aled or Kevin who picked him up was negotiable. But after a whole weekend *and* this morning with Aled, Gabriel fancied a change of pace.

And Kevin was expecting him, because the reply came back within seconds.

Kevin: On my way.

Gabriel lounged by the door, smoking and talking to the security guard about the possibility of the store closing down. It was threatening to snow. Gabriel wasn't really one for Christmas—he usually had to spend it making awkward small talk with his grandfather and uncles in Pudsey, instead of on his back with someone ploughing him like a field as he would have preferred—but a white Christmas was tempting. Leeds was pretty in the snow. Even Wakefield looked nice. It had snowed on Aled's birthday last year, and he'd fucked Gabriel in a snowdrift. It had bloody hurt and been bloody fantastic to boot.

Kevin's banger of a car pulled up into a proper parking spot, and Gabriel worked his way through another cigarette as Kevin did a quick circuit. Typical mid-week emergency supplies of a family man, even if Kevin looked more like a mob enforcer than anyone's dad. The basket gave him away. Nappies, milk and a pack of burgers.

"Burgers?" Gabriel asked when he came back out.

"Grace is having a phase," Kevin said, and rolled his eyes.

Kevin was a big man. Big shoulders, big chest, big dick. When Kevin fucked him, Gabriel could feel it for a week. Even gentle handling from someone with hands like Kevin's felt dangerous. When he leaned over for a kiss in the car, Gabriel felt like any wrong move would leave a bruise on his jaw — even though Kevin was barely touching him.

He shivered and pressed harder into the kiss.

"You want the basement after all?" Kevin rumbled.

"Too sore," Gabriel admitted. "Maybe next week?"

"No problem."

They didn't talk again on the way over. The silence was comfortable. Gabriel surfed radio channels, Kevin drove and they ignored each other peacefully enough until the garage door closed behind him and plunged them into darkness.

Then Gabriel jumped as a hand was pushed insistently down the front of his jeans.

"Too sore, huh?"

"Um — inside. Too — too sore inside."

"Then you shouldn't have been sucking on my tongue like a slut, should you?"

Gabriel whined. He lifted his hips as Kevin's fingers pushed farther back, and began to ride the heel of his palm. A single finger forced its way inside, and he whimpered at the painful scratch of a jagged nail edge.

"Keep your mouth shut, or I'll fuck your arse instead."

Oh, *fuck*. Gabriel clamped his own hand over his mouth. It had been far too long since Kevin's deep threats, and now he had to be finger-fucked in silence? That was just —

The nail caught. Pain blossomed. Blood poured south, and he rutted into Kevin's palm like a horny virgin.

"F-fuck — "

Gabriel's face hit the dashboard. He bit his tongue. Tasted blood. He was cupped between both hands, one down the front and one down the back, then—

"Fuck-fuck-fuck-*fuck*—!"

Another nail. Dry. Pushing. *Forcing*—

"One more word out of you and it *will* be a fuck."

He gasped wordlessly as he was probed. The jagged nails hurt. The blunt stabs of movement ached. And the constant moving pressure of Kevin's palm against his cock, rubbing and rubbing and *rubbing*—

Then it stopped.

Air. The tightening frenzy began to fade. The high sank.

But he was still there. One finger in his arse and two in his cunt. Being cut open from the inside by rough nails. Pinned.

Waiting.

Gabriel could sense the danger. He knew the next step. If he spoke again, Kevin would fuck him properly. Shove that thick prick in him and fuck until he bled. Fill him up. Then if he was feeling *really* sadistic, fist him. Plunge the cum and the blood right back out of him on Kevin's fist—

His cock strained. It ached. It *wanted*.

He licked his lips—and Kevin spoke.

"What do I get if I let you come?"

Silence.

"Seems only fair that I get something out of it."

More silence.

"Don't you agree?"

Gabriel felt the sweat running down the back of his neck.

And another finger pushed at his arse.

"Don't."

Pain crackled up his spine as it entered him.

"You."

Deeper.

"Agree?"

"Y-yes, sir."

The fingers stilled.

"That's better."

Kevin's voice was very low. Deeper than the darkness in the garage and twice as frightening. Gabriel shivered as fear and lust wound around one another in his brain into a tangled weave.

"You wanted a kiss earlier."

It sounded like a change of subject, but Gabriel knew better. He whimpered.

"If your cock gets to come, only fair that mine does. And you can have all the kisses you want while you're fucking it. Sound fair?"

"Y-yes, sir."

"After you."

Gabriel groaned when the fingers started to fuck him again. And it wasn't slow and torturous anymore. It was fast. A proper fuck. It hurt. He could feel blood from Kevin's fingernails. And when they caught at the exact same time, and *dragged*—

He came.

Came.

Fucked Kevin's palm like he'd not had sex in a year. White-out. Air like icicles inside. Shook apart. *Came.*

Came so hard that—

That then—

Gabriel came back to himself muzzily. He felt heavy. Lethargic. Almost drunk. His jeans were gone. His hips ached. Bruises on the outside and a dick like hot steel inside. Fucking. In and out and in again. He relaxed on it. Sagged against Kevin's shirt, hips being smashed down between those huge hands, just—limp. Being fucked like a doll. A toy. A plaything.

He ducked his head against Kevin's jaw. Nudged. A mouth swallowed his own, all teeth and tongue and *heat*.

When he was flooded, it felt like being washed from the ocean to an island that was home.

When he was pushed back against the steering wheel and inspected, it was like being studied as a work of art.

And when he was fisted and the cum punched right back out, it should have felt like agonising torture.

Instead, it felt like being anchored back to shore.

* * * *

"There you are!" Judith trilled when he came back downstairs from the shower. "I thought you might have fallen in the toilet and drowned!"

Gabriel just grinned at the sight in front of him.

From being fucked and fisted in Kevin's car to *this*? Really?

It was nearly seven, and the whole house smelled of dinner. Kevin was sprawled on the sofa, three-year-old Grace snoring against his left shoulder and four-year-old Lily against his right. Judith was tucked up in the armchair, breastfeeding their newest addition and cooing every time a chubby hand waved.

"Ooh, new baby!" Gabriel enthused.

He skipped right past Kevin and hunkered down by Judith to peer at the new baby. He didn't know anything. They hadn't found out before the birth what it was and all Kevin had said was 'healthy baby' in his texts.

"What's its name?" Gabriel asked, touching a little fist and earning himself a surprised blink. Its complexion was closer to Judith's than Kevin's, and Gabriel guessed it would be a lot paler than Lily and Grace, but the fuzzy darkness haloing its head said that Kevin's cornrow-captured locks had won the genetic battle for dominance for the third time.

"She," Judith said peaceably. "Another girl. I want a boy next."

"Who said anything about next?" Kevin groused.

"I did," she returned tartly.

"You're mad," Kevin said seriously and heaved himself up. His abs flexed under his obscenely tight T-shirt and were strong enough to haul him and both girls up without pause. "I'll get these two down. You and Gabriel get eating. I'll join you in a bit."

"How you doing?" Judith asked.

Gabriel winced. "I was sore when I got here, and I'm even worse now, thanks to your husband."

She laughed. "Well, he's not allowed near me and he says Sophie's had quite enough of him for a while."

"I'm not surprised!"

They bitched and moaned about Kevin's truncheon of a dick until the baby was done, then Gabriel was allowed to cuddle her and try to coax a burp out of her. She still smelled like new baby and she was a heavy lump of happiness against his skin. Aled might hate children, but Gabriel liked them just fine. At least when they were snoring and sweet, anyway.

"Did you pick a name?" he asked.

"Yup. You want spaghetti?"

He rolled his eyes. "Fine, don't tell me."

He followed her into the kitchen and stood at the sink with the baby while she rustled up plates. The chaos from feeding the other two was still evident, but Judith moved around it all with practised ease. When Kevin came back down, they were both shooed to sit down and he took over.

It was comfortable.

It was home, even though Gabriel had never lived with them. Judith drew the line at having her husband's other subs actually in her living space, but he was always invited for dinner, always allowed to stay the night if he needed it or pop round for a brew. He even babysat occasionally when they needed a break and Kevin wasn't on speaking terms with Judith's mum for the umpteenth time.

He'd never lived here and yet it was home.

"Right," Kevin said, banging the plates down. "Swap you this for that. I'll pop her up in her crib."

"Nope," Gabriel said, nuzzling his jaw against the baby's head. She'd fallen asleep, a fist clamped around the collar of his polo shirt. "Not until you tell me her name. If I have to name her, then I'm keeping her."

Kevin chuckled.

"You won't like it," Judith said. "You'll get embarrassed and won't talk to us all evening."

"It can't be that—"

"Gabrielle."

Gabriel shut up.

He handed the baby back.

And he didn't say another word, just flushed brilliantly red and mumbled throughout the rest of the meal.

Chapter Five

"Drink?" Suze suggested as they reconvened at the gym's cafe. "Tom's at a stag do, and I'll get a right bollocking if I dare start a new boxset without him."

"Sorry," Aled said, rummaging in his pockets for his car keys and trailing in her wake to the door, "but I'm going round to Gabriel's. Going to talk to him about this Michael situation. He went round Kevin's after work yesterday so he should be in a good mood."

Suze squeezed Aled's arm as they reached their cars. "Good luck. And handle it *delicately*. Do not, whatever you do, make him think you're going to be cutting off all of his regulars!"

"Are you kidding? I'd have to take over what Kevin does and no fucking thank you. I've seen those videos."

Despite her encouragement and knowing he had no choice but to discuss the issue before it became an outright problem, Aled still felt nervous as he drove up to Belle Isle. Gabriel could be a touch unpredictable with his wariness. He would let Aled kidnap him, tie him up, role-play torture and rape, hostage situations and slavery — and yet sometimes he would slam the brakes on about something so small as Aled paying for dinner. They had to extensively negotiate every single time Aled wanted to film him, even though Aled kept the films for his personal use only and Kevin, one of Gabriel's other regulars, put them up on the internet as homemade porn. And he would sometimes let Aled lock him in Aled's bathroom, chained to the radiator and gagged, for entire weekends — and sometimes, he would bolt at the mere suggestion of staying over for a week.

So Gabriel was either going to cheerfully agree and bin off Michael without batting an eyelash, or he was going to go absolutely ballistic.

It was late, black as midnight, as Aled pulled up outside the flats. The lights were on in Gabriel's. He jogged up the stairs, hoping Gabriel wasn't busy with someone else, but when he knocked, he heard a TV programme suddenly pause and the distinct shuffle of bare feet on carpet.

"Aled!"

Gabriel offered a quick peck on the cheek before letting him in. He was dressed for a lazy evening in, wearing nothing but a T-shirt so large and baggy that it could have served as a dress. His hair was wet and when Aled closed the front door behind himself and ducked in for another, longer kiss, he could smell limes.

"Fresh out the shower?"

"Yep," Gabriel said, smiling against his cheek and running his nails down Aled's jaw lightly before stepping back. "What's brought you here?"

"Just — wanted to see you," Aled said, deciding to go in gently. He offered a hug and, on a whim, hoisted

Gabriel up and spun him in a circle before dropping him again. "Had dinner yet?"

"Dinner yes, dessert no. Ice cream and telly?"

"Please."

"You staying the night?"

"If that's all right? I'll just to go work straight from here, if you don't mind."

There was a drawer full of Aled's clothes now, although he hoped to persuade Gabriel to move down to Wakefield with him rather than come up here to Belle Isle. He didn't fancy living in such a shit part of Leeds and had never liked Gabriel doing so either.

"Fine by me, but if I don't get at least a *sighting* of that cock of yours for an overnight visit, I'll be upset," Gabriel teased.

Aled rolled his eyes, leaning a hip against the sofa as Gabriel headed for the kitchenette to check on the food situation.

"How's Kevin?"

"Oh my God," Gabriel muttered. "They only went and did it."

"Did what?"

"You know what they've called the new baby?"

"We don't really talk unless it's about you," Aled admitted.

"Gabby."

"Oh, that's ni—"

"As in Gabrielle."

Aled laughed at the colour flooding Gabriel's cheeks. But when Gabriel didn't join in, it trailed off. He frowned.

"Is that—that's not your deadname, is it?"

Gabriel blinked.

Then flushed even more darkly. "Oh, God! No-no-no-no. Kevin knows better than that. No, just—*really*? Gabrielle? They named their *baby* after me!"

"They're practically your family, of course they did," Aled said dismissively. "Face it. You have family."

Gabriel whined in an exaggerated manner.

"You'll be lucky if Suze doesn't name one after you too. I've already had to persuade her to use Alex instead of Aled if she has a son."

"She's banned."

"Good luck with that," Aled said dryly.

"I'll change mine again," Gabriel insisted, bending down to open the freezer. The shirt-dress rode up—and Aled froze.

A deep bruise, a bite-mark, was visible on Gabriel's arse.

Fresh.

His eyes flickered over Gabriel's skin and found another just peeking out of the neckline of the T-shirt. There was a shadow on his wrist, too, perhaps from a hand.

Jealousy flashed, rising like a solar flare, hot and bright in his chest. Michael had been here. Kevin's were bigger. Darker. *More.* And if it were a stranger, Gabriel wouldn't have permitted bites that deep.

Michael had been there.

Aled balled his hands into fists and forced down the aggression. They'd not talked about it. Gabriel hadn't betrayed him. He'd done nothing wrong. It was just—just a regular. Just another regular. Just Michael.

Just Michael.

Gabriel turned from the freezer and stilled. Slowly, he leaned back against the counter, knees parting, elbows rising to rest on the granite behind him and tow the shirt-dress gently upwards, exposing long, bare thighs. One of them was bruised. A handprint.

"Like what you see?" he whispered.

"No," Aled returned, voice hard. "There's marks. Where've you picked up teeth and hands on your skin?"

Gabriel toyed with the neck of the T-shirt, dropping his eyes. "The hands were Kevin last night."

"And?"

"And—and Michael came over," he breathed. "I was alone. He's not you, but—"

Aled crossed the room in three strides and seized Gabriel by the throat. Gabriel gasped, stiffening, and Aled raised his hand a little higher, forcing Gabriel up onto his tiptoes.

"No, he's not me," he said. "You've let someone touch you that isn't me. Do you think that's right?"

"N-no, sir."

"Why not?"

"I—I'm yours, sir." Gabriel's eyes were nearly black with lust, his voice beginning to shake. "I belong to you. I—I should only open my legs for other men if you tell me to."

"And did I?"

"No, sir."

"I think you need reminding of your place," Aled said smoothly. "Take off my belt."

Gabriel swallowed, his throat bobbing against Aled's palm, and dropped his hands. He fumbled clumsily with Aled's belt, sliding it out of the loops, and when it was out, placed it into Aled's free hand.

"Please, sir, don't beat me," he whispered.

They'd been playing long enough that Aled heard the veiled warning, and he rubbed the leather across Gabriel's lips.

"You *do* need reminding," he sneered. "It's not your place to make demands. It's mine to give orders. And yours to obey them. No matter what they are."

Without warning, he slid his hand around to the back of Gabriel's neck, twisted and propelled him forward to the sofa, shoving him down on his knees in front of it and pinning his upper body by the neck to the cushions. Then he wrenched both arms up behind Gabriel's back and tied them together with the belt.

"Your place," Aled grunted, resting his full weight onto Gabriel's bound arms and drawing out his own cock with his free hand, "is on your knees, with your mouth and legs open. For me. *Just* me."

"Y-yes, sir."

"What do you want?"

"You t-to remind me, sir. To fuck me, sir."

"You deserve that, do you?" Aled mused, pressing the head of his swollen cock to Gabriel's arse. Slowly, he dragged it down to the other opening, then back up. Shallow, teasing strokes. Threatening ones — because he was still completely dry.

"No, sir."

"No, you're right." He felt the tell-tale looseness, the traces of smoothness indicating lube at the front, and settled there. "What are you?"

"A sheath for your cock."

"What are you?"

"A body for you to fuck."

"What. Are. You."

Gabriel's voice shuddered. "*Yours.*"

Aled pushed.

Dry, he forced his way into a wet, clinging tightness, already used but already keen for more. Gabriel cried out but clenched down and pulled all the same, opening up and drawing Aled deeper. It was like wet silk, satin-smooth and intensely hot, and Aled began to thrust without giving Gabriel time to adjust. In long, powerful strokes, he drove Gabriel into the cushions, ploughing him, using him, *fucking* in the basest sense of the word.

Gabriel writhed, gasping and whimpering. He rutted against the sofa, seeking pressure, seeking pleasure, and Aled forced more weight down onto those bound arms until new bruises bloomed. Reaching under, he started to grind and twist Gabriel's flesh between finger and thumb, torturing him until he yelled, stilling when Gabriel's thigh shivered with the beginnings of a climax — and started again when the danger passed, until Gabriel was nothing but incoherent begging, limp and helpless, under him.

Only when Aled's balls tightened and his vision dimmed did he pull out and drag Gabriel to the floor, twisting him over and shoving his cock into that slack, pleading mouth. He came messily, Gabriel choking on the sudden flood of it, cum spilling over his lips and chin. Aled laughed, rubbing the spent head across his lips, then seized his hair and pulled his head back against the cushions, long neck exposed.

"You like this, don't you?" Aled hissed, rubbing his lips along Gabriel's neck, tasting salt where his cum had spilled. He rubbed his fingers against Gabriel's wet dick too, but his position between Gabriel's spread legs prevented his caught toy from closing his legs and rubbing himself off. "Legs open, covered in someone else's pleasure, held down and ready to be used."

Gabriel was breathing harshly, eyes black and wide and dazed. He was barely there and Aled rubbed his thumb slowly over the head of that swollen cock, even as he pushed three fingers at once into the well-fucked passage.

The climax hit. He squeezed and massaged through it, the pressure almost enough to break his fingers, Gabriel's shuddering almost convulsive — then a shiver passed over his face, the most beautiful bliss that Aled had ever seen, and Aled's breath caught in his lungs.

"God," he breathed, and kissed Gabriel's throat when it was over, releasing his hair. "You look so *beautiful*."

Suddenly, an intense sense of shame washed over him. He fumbled with the belt, slipping it free and discarding it to one side, not wanting to see it. He had come over to talk reasonably about this jealousy issue. Instead, the sight of a single hickey had him dragging Gabriel down to the sofa and using him like a whore, saying he was *owned* —

Gabriel's arms looped around his neck, cutting off Aled's thoughts, and his lips, wet and sticky, brushed along Aled's cheek.

"'Mazing," he whispered throatily. "God, that was amazing."

"You okay?" Aled breathed, resting his hands cautiously on Gabriel's wrist, over the sweat-soaked shirt.

"'Mazing," Gabriel repeated. His eyes were still foggy, but the smile was wide and peaceful. "That was — love you."

Aled's heart staggered.

"I do," Gabriel murmured. "Was all passion and fire and *you*..."

Aled swallowed, and nuzzled at Gabriel's ear, slowly daring to hug him back. Gabriel's thighs, still spread over Aled's knees, slid up and locked around his waist until he was almost in his lap.

"Not too much?" Aled dared.

"God, not *enough,*" Gabriel breathed, gnawing at Aled's shoulder almost absently. "Stay the night. Ice cream, and showers, then — then tie me to the bed, proper bolt me down so I can't even move, and can you fuck me again like that? Like you're a *machine*? God, I thought you were going to split me in half, it was *incredible…*"

Aled hoisted them bodily onto the sofa, curling up under Gabriel's form until they were cuddled together, too-hot and covered in body fluids, Gabriel's skin sticky and almost clammy under his hands.

And breathed. Gabriel like this, nuzzling into him and whispering for more of the same, brushed off Aled's fears like as though they were nothing. They *were* nothing. Gabriel had played along. Gabriel wanted to play along some more. And he had issued that warning, that veiled threat of a word. The *how* was more than fine.

Aled's anxiety settled, mollified, and he smoothed down Gabriel's hair, pressing that dark head into his shoulder for a moment, before kissing his forehead and sighing softly.

"Ice cream and showers," he whispered.

"You okay?"

"Yeah. Yeah. Just — yeah."

Gabriel's arms tightened. His lips grazed the top of Aled's shoulder.

"Need some aftercare?"

Aled closed his eyes. Gratitude bubbled up inside, warm and soft and smoothing over the jagged edges left by the searing heat of his aggression.

"Yeah," he murmured.

Gabriel squeezed. "What do you need?"

"This. You. Cuddle. Ice cream and a shower."

"Deal."

"And if you're really bad, another reminder."

Gabriel laughed, and it was the most effective balm in the world. Aled relaxed, rocked their heads together gently, and the final traces of anxiety eased. It was fine. It had been fun. And —

And they could talk about the *why* later.

Chapter Six

Something was wrong with Aled.

Gabriel wasn't stupid. Aled could—did—get aggressive when he wanted to fuck, and it was why they'd started out on this relationship in the first place. But it wasn't usually so sudden. He liked to build up to it. He liked to play games with plenty of warning, not just launch from 'how's Kevin?' to fucking a cheating slut on the sofa.

Frankly, Gabriel wasn't surprised Aled had needed some aftercare.

He'd stayed the night and there'd been no more sex. Just cuddling and lounging around in jogging bottoms. Gabriel had ripped the piss out of some shit sci-fi Aled had wanted to watch and woken up around three in the morning when Aled had come back to bed from the bathroom and wrapped himself around Gabriel like a touch-deprived squid. Less slimy, but Gabriel swore the man grew extra limbs in the night.

He'd not asked—but then Aled had told him anyway.

"I need to get something off my chest," he'd admitted, halfway into his clothes the next morning. "Can I come over tonight? We can go get something to eat and talk it out."

"What do we need to talk about?" Gabriel had asked warily.

"Nothing bad. Promise."

So Gabriel had agreed, earned himself a sweet kiss at the door and that had been that. But frankly, the anticipation had nagged all day, so he feigned a stomach-ache and left work an hour early, intending to have a shower, tidy the flat and brace himself for whatever had gotten Aled so wound up.

Then—just as he put the key in the door—he heard the voice.

"Hell-o, beautiful. Come to Daddy."

Gabriel wheeled around at the catcall and laughed. He'd have to brace for something else entirely—Michael was grinning at him from the stairs.

"I mean it, bring that pretty little arse over here," Michael continued, beaming widely. He'd started growing in a beard and it made his wide, dentist-advert smile even filthier.

But Gabriel wasn't in the mood to play it easy. Michael had come over yesterday afternoon. They'd fucked. The edge had been taken off. So now the git could work for it.

"Why would I want to have my arse anywhere near a random bloke hanging out in the stairwell by my flat?" Gabriel asked, turning back and unlocking his front door.

He didn't even finish turning the key before Michael was up against his back, pressing him into the door and reaching around to unbutton his jeans.

"Because I've got a fucking foot-long dick that's hard enough to hammer nails into walls, and it wants to hammer *you*."

Gabriel groaned as nimble fingers shoved their way into his briefs, pushed his packer out of the way and began to massage him. Shivers flickered up his spine and fire lapped at his crotch as Michael tugged at him, thrusting against his arse in time with his fingers.

"Pull 'em down and let me watch my cum drip down your legs, yeah, baby?"

Gabriel twisted the key and jerked the door open. They tumbled into his flat and he was slammed up against the door again, Michael licking a stripe up the side of his face before roughly pulling his jeans and pants down and beginning to finger him.

"Front or back?" Michael grunted in his ear, grinding against his thigh. "Won't have no lube, though. Too far gone to touch it."

Oh, Christ, that would hurt, then. Michael's dick wasn't nearly as long as he said it was, but it was a thick bastard. Obscenely thick. It was like being fucked with a bottle — and not the neck, either.

"Then come on my face," Gabriel breathed, "and by the time you've opened me up enough to take you deep, you'll be ready again."

"No, need it inside. *Now*."

Gabriel grimaced, resigning himself to a bit of a brutal fuck — although at least it would be short — and said, "Front, then. Can't take *that* without lube in the back."

Michael laughed and licked him again before kissing him, slack and open-mouthed, gasping with desperate intent into his mouth as he fumbled with his own jeans, the bulge in them making it difficult.

Then the door bounced behind Gabriel's ear as someone knocked heavily.

"Forget it," Michael hissed, mouth moving to bite and chew at Gabriel's neck, messy and wet. "Won't be nobody important."

The next knock was a flat bang—a palm slap—and Gabriel groaned, knowing who it was. And knowing that, really, he shouldn't be here just yet. He was too early. He must have skipped work too.

"Let me just—"

"*Leave it!*" Michael insisted, seizing Gabriel's wrist when he tried to reach the handle. Gabriel scowled, a surge of anger rising at the display, and he shoved, pushing Michael off him. He pulled his briefs up, stepping out of his work slacks entirely, and opened the door in nothing but his rumpled Tesco polo shirt and Primark underwear, with a liberal amount of spit on his face and neck.

Aled *stared*.

"Fuck's sake, babe," Michael said over his shoulder, then dropped an arm across the back of his neck, leaning forward to talk to Aled. "Sorry, mate, look, we're busy, heard all the great news about God, thanks, bye."

He pushed the door. Gabriel stuck his foot in it and shrugged the arm off.

"Ignore him," he told Aled pointedly. "Is everything okay?"

"Er—no. No, not—not really. I was, uh. Hoping we could talk sooner rather than later."

Aled never took his eyes off Michael, and a chill crept up Gabriel's spine.

"Right now?"

"If you're not—otherwise engaged."

"He is, so come back in, say, ten minutes?" Michael interrupted.

Ten minutes? Gabriel snorted. Enough for Michael to shove his dick inside him, come, slap his thigh and walk out. No way would *Gabriel* get any real fun out of it in ten minutes, not with a man who refused to give oral anywhere near a vagina.

"Michael, shove off. Use your hand if you're that desperate. Aled, sorry, I just got back from work, you can come in if you want or we can go somewhere —"

"Are you serious?" Michael said.

"Very, piss off."

Aled was glancing between them, a dark expression on his face. Michael huffed, an angry scowl crossing his, but then he shoved past and stormed out without a backward glance, gait awkward.

"What did I interrupt," Aled asked flatly.

"Michael with blue balls," Gabriel replied and gestured for him to come in. "He was about to come in his pants. Or mine."

"Right," Aled said and frowned harder. "He seemed — aggressive."

"Most men are when they get stopped from shooting off with five seconds to spare," Gabriel said tartly then shrugged. "I'm not fussed. It's his problem. Didn't sound like I was going to get too much from it anyway."

"Why?"

"He was at the shove-it-in-and-shoot stage. And he's *wide*. It would have hurt and I would have only got a hand to help me. He doesn't do oral."

"He's an idiot. Eating you out is amazing," Aled said flatly. He shucked his jacket off and offered a quick kiss. "Still, I should have called ahead. I just—really needed to talk to you, so I took off after my meeting."

"Talk about what?"

"Well—"

There was a long pause, during which Gabriel just waited and Aled got redder and redder, rubbing the back of his neck.

"Him."

Gabriel frowned. "What, Michael?"

"Yeah." Aled was starting to go maroon, a mottled flush creeping up his neck.

"Is...everything okay?"

"I—no. Not really."

Aled dropped to sit on Gabriel's sofa, and Gabriel hesitated. He was torn between getting mad and getting worried. Aled was usually good at talking. This reticence was odd and Gabriel felt thrown by it.

"Um—do you want a cup of tea or something?"

"No. No, just...come and sit here? I need to talk and it's not something I'm proud of and it's—it's up to you how we deal with it."

Warily, Gabriel perched on the cushions. Aled reached out and plucked his hand from his knee, cupping it both of his own and beginning to massage the fingers. It felt nice, but also very strange in and of itself.

"I'm just going to say it," Aled said, and sighed. "I'm jealous of Michael."

Gabriel's blood ran cold.

"I'm getting angry when I know he's touched you. I'm upset when you talk about him. I'm finding myself unable to touch you gently if Michael's been around. I feel like I have to dominate you, almost like I'm staking a claim—"

Slowly, Gabriel drew his hand back, his heart pounding. Shit. *Shit.* He had a jealous dominant on his hands, a jealous dominant who was built for monogamy —

"But it's just him."

Gabriel's growing panic…paused.

"I'm not having the same reaction to Kevin. Or your random hook-ups. It's just Michael."

The panic receded a little.

"Why just him?"

Aled blew upwards into his hair and took off his glasses to rub at his eyes. He looked tired, suddenly older than his thirty-four years.

"I talked it over with Suze," he said, "and she thinks it's because he's — I — fuck. I think he's a dick. To you. And I don't — you know I love you."

Gabriel did know that, but it didn't stop the little hiccup that his heart made.

"I think I'm struggling with leaving you in the hands of someone who — who just sees you as an object. As a warm hole to shove his prick into."

Gabriel licked his lips. "So do several of my one-night stands."

"Yeah, but that's a one-time thing. He's not."

"It's not really any of your business how Michael sees me, Aled."

"No, I know," Aled said quickly. He dragged a hand through his hair until it stood up in spiky ginger clumps. "I think — he unsettles me. The way he is with you."

"Like — ?"

"I know this is pretty rich coming from me, given what we do, but — from my perspective, he just looks like he uses you."

"How?"

"Like the other day when I found his hickeys. And just now. He's stormed off in a paddy. You said he was at the shove-it-in stage, that it would hurt and he'd not really get you off after. And the texts he sends you sometimes—look, I know it's hypocritical of me and I know there's plenty we do that would be seen by an outsider to be that way, but...he unsettles me. I get the feeling he's only around because he sees you as a sex object."

Gabriel raised his eyebrows. "He's forward, I'll give you that—"

"I'm not saying I'm right, Gabe—"

" —riel, Christ!"

" —but that's why he's disturbing me, I think. I don't like him, and I don't trust him with you."

"Right," Gabriel said. "So you're jealous of him."

"Maybe not quite *of him*, but I act like a jealous twat when he's around, yeah. It's like—it's like when you had to introduce me and Kevin because I thought he was abusing you last year. It's like then. You had to—I don't know, I guess prove to me that he wasn't a cunt. Only *that*"—he gestured at the closed front door—"that was a cunt."

Gabriel eyed the door.

Then let out a low, long breath. And inhaled. Took his hand back from Aled and twisted them around each other.

"What do you want me to do about it?"

Aled blinked then reached for Gabriel's hand again. Gabriel let him take it.

"It's your choice. It always is. But I would—"

Another long pause yawned between them.

" —prefer it if he weren't around."

"At all?"

"At all."

Shit.

"You want me to dump him."

Aled squirmed. "Well…yeah."

Gabriel pursed his lips. "Aled. I'm not going monogamous for you. Or anybody else."

"I'm not asking that. I swear I'm not." Aled's fingers tightened around Gabriel's. "I—I've never been bothered by your hook-ups. And I like your games with Kevin. The videos are fucking fantastic—"

Gabriel cracked a wary smile.

"—but there's something about *him*. Just him. And I think—I think it is that combination, rather than it's someone you fancy, or someone who fancies you. That Danny kid who won't stop messaging you on Grindr obviously fancies you, but he doesn't bother me."

"He's also not slept with me."

Aled sighed heavily, raking a hand through his hair.

"I can't—I can't pin it down," he admitted. "I only have Michael to go from, and that one time with Kevin. I honestly—I honestly don't know if this is a one-off, it's-just-him issue, or whether there's going to be problems with other emotional regulars, but in my defence, he's been around longer than me and it's only recently I'm having these issues with him."

"So why now?" Gabriel pressed. He felt uneasy and pulled away entirely, getting up and going to the kitchenette under the pretence of getting a glass of water. He didn't want to have this conversation. He didn't want Aled to get jealous of other men, because if he did, then it would only be a matter of time before he started trying to curtail Gabriel's activities with other guys. Then Gabriel would have to run, or be pinned down under an angry, jealous dominant with far too much control over his life.

And *God*, he didn't want that to be Aled.

Aled hesitated, then said, "Those texts over your birthday weekend."

"Sorry?"

"He—he texted you something like, *you need to finish up your party and get back here, I need a decent shag with your arse at the end of it*. And it was just…urgh."

"You've texted me things like that."

"I love you."

The confession was frank and forthright and Gabriel resisted the urge to glance down. Twice in one conversation? Aled had only started saying it recently and Gabriel wasn't used to hearing it.

"Maybe Michael loves me."

"Maybe he does. And that's what I mean—I *know* there's things I say to you, things I do to you, that he'd be equally justified in using to paint me as some complete dickhead, but—I just get a nasty vibe off him and I don't want him near you. So I'm finding myself angry and jealous when I know he's been around and I don't want to be. I *really* don't. And I don't have this problem with Kevin, or with any of your Grindr guys—"

Except he had had that problem with Kevin. And now he was having it with Michael. And Gabriel wasn't liking the pattern that was trying to emerge.

"So what do you want me to do," he repeated flatly, folding his arms over his chest.

"Why do you sleep with him?"

Gabriel didn't miss a beat. "He's a Greek god with a dick that can rip me inside out."

"So you don't—love him."

"I fancy him. As long as he looks like that."

"But it's not— You don't want to date him."

"No."

Aled swallowed. "Then…is he replaceable?"

Gabriel frowned. "You want me to replace him?"

"I want to know if it's *him*. And I think it is. Kevin cares for you and, hell, I *like* that he cares for you. I don't mind when you say you fancy people you've been playing with. And if it just Michael, then—then what's the problem?"

"The problem is it's the second time you've gotten twitchy about one of my other men. And okay, we sorted it out with Kevin. But you're not asking to sort this out—you're asking me to dump Michael completely. And if I give in to this, then you'll ask again. And again and again, until I'm not allowed to play with *anyone* else and—"

"I won't."

Gabriel narrowed his eyes.

"I *won't*," Aled insisted, his eyes wide and imploring. "I was married for *years* and my wife certainly loved a couple of guys who weren't me. And I never got jealous. I'm not asking for monogamy. I'm *not*. I'm just asking for Michael to not be one of the others."

A little relaxation eased into Gabriel's shoulders, though he maintained his firm stance against the counter.

"She loved other people? Really loved them? Melissa?"

"Yeah. I only got jealous near the end, when I could feel she didn't love me anymore."

Slowly, Aled came up off the sofa and padded across the carpet, cupping Gabriel's elbows between his hands and rubbing at them lightly. His face was open. Relaxed. There was nothing hiding behind the eyes.

"But I know you love me. You don't say it much and you're still skittish of the whole commitment thing sometimes, but I *know*."

Gabriel swallowed, nodding awkwardly.

"And I think as long as I know that, as long as I know that the other guys are *in addition* to me, not *instead of* me, then I'll be okay. I really do think it's Michael being a cunt to you."

"He's never hurt me."

"Yeah, well, maybe you're comfortable with a guy coming round to stick his dick in you, shoot off and leave again without so much as kissing you, but I'm not."

Gabriel coughed a brief laugh and called Aled a romantic.

"No, I just know what sex should be, and that's for both parties."

"He's not some john, Aled."

"He could easily be," Aled parried, and slid his arms a little farther around Gabriel's waist in a loose hug, eyeing him from close range. "So — would you?"

"Get rid of Michael because my dominant, self-professed boyfriend doesn't like him?"

"And promises it's *just* Michael and if he starts having problems with *any* of the rest of it then he won't say a word and will — will go to counselling to deal with his stupid, egotistical emotions?"

Gabriel frowned. "Promise?"

"I swear," Aled said gravely. "If it turns out it's not just Michael, I will go to counselling and we will sort it out *without* you changing your lifestyle. I said it at the beginning and I'll say it now. I don't *want* you to belong to me. I want you to belong to me in *scenes*, when we're *playing*, then to switch it all off and be *you*. And 'you' is a flighty, sex-mad socialite who could turn a priest."

Gabriel chewed on his lip. He wanted to believe it. He wanted to focus on the aftercare last night, on the way Aled would cuddle up in the kitchen if they were making dinner together, the blanket on his sofa at the house in Wakefield where they'd squash up on the cushions and Gabriel would make fun of Aled's taste in TV shows —

But the other side of him was there too. The dominant who'd fucked Gabriel over the sofa because another man had been round. The master who'd kidnapped him for his birthday and pretended to punish him for the better part of three days for getting messages from other men.

What if he turned?

But what if he didn't?

Gabriel had fixed the problem with Kevin. Once Aled had realised Gabriel *wanted* Kevin to hit him sometimes, he'd been fine. He'd never tried to stand between them since. And — and that was the moment, wasn't it?

That was the moment that Gabriel had fallen in love with Aled for real.

Back in the summer, Aled had wanted to play a long game. They'd never played *long* before and Aled wanted to try it out. He'd wanted to lock Gabriel in the spare room and train him for sex. It was a game from one of their favourite porn films and one Gabriel had been itching to try out. And — out of nowhere — Aled had suggested it.

"Two weeks," he'd said. "You take some time off work, and we play. All the usual rules, you can safeword anything or the whole thing, but I'd just like to try it."

"I can't," Gabriel had said. "Not more than a week. I have to stay in touch with Kevin."

So Aled had made it happen. Every day of the game, Aled had allowed Gabriel ten minutes of free use of his phone. Ten minutes when Aled had just left the room, let Gabriel make the call or send his messages, then had come back and taken it away — and never looked.

He'd never once looked at what Gabriel was saying.

He hadn't *cared*.

And that was the moment that Gabriel had thought that he might actually love Aled a bit. That was the man he wanted to trust. That was the man he wanted to hold on to. That was the man he loved. He'd done it once. He'd been angry with Kevin in the beginning and they'd fixed it. Then that long game — he'd helped Gabriel meet the rules. And he'd never checked what Gabriel had said.

Not ever.

Gabriel swallowed.

He'd trusted him when he'd asked to prove Kevin wasn't dangerous. He'd trusted him when he'd introduced Aled to Kevin properly. He'd trusted him in that game to not break Kevin's rules on Gabriel's behalf. And he could trust him again now.

Right?

"He comes round a lot."

Aled blinked. "What?"

"Michael. And it takes time to set up new regulars."

"So —"

"So either there's going to be a *lot* of hook-ups and less time for you, what with going out to meet them and everything, or you're going to have to step up to the plate."

Aled smirked. "I'll step up."

"You sure you can handle that?"

A hand ghosted down to cup Gabriel's backside through his briefs and squeeze. "I'll manage. It's not exactly like screwing you is a chore."

"If you can't step up, then you don't get to complain about me going out to find others."

"I won't," Aled promised. "Never do, except for Michael."

Gabriel exhaled, then nodded. "Okay."

"Okay—?"

"Okay, I'll break it off with him. But I mean it, Aled, this is the *one* time you get to ask this. I *do* love you, but I'm not sacrificing all other men for you, especially not with your dominant tendencies."

Aled's arms tightened and he squeezed tightly in a hug, hooking his chin over Gabriel's shoulder and rocking them lightly. It was tight. Warm. Comfortable—but not quite comforting. Gabriel rested his cheek against the closest shoulder but didn't quite relax.

"That's fine," Aled whispered. "More than fine. That's *good*. And I promise, I *swear*, this is the only time I'll ask. If I'm wrong, if it's about regulars and not Michael, then not only will I not say a word if you get back with him, but I will find a counsellor and we will iron out my emotions together and stop the issue in its tracks. *Promise*."

Gabriel squeezed back, settling his head on Aled's shoulder, and hoped he wasn't misplacing his trust. In Aled, *or* Michael.

Because Michael was not going to like this.

Chapter Seven

Aled was nervous.

All right, Gabriel had agreed to break it off with Michael — but Aled was still twitchy. Afraid it would happen again. Scared he'd be wrong and it wouldn't be just Michael but slowly dissolve into any other guy who Gabriel looked at with that wide open expression. Because that face — the one he gave Aled, the one he had when he talked about Kevin — wasn't his predatory, sex-mad face.

It was his *heart.*

And Aled was scared that he was going to start hating it being directed at anyone but himself.

Still, he clung to the simple fact that Gabriel pulled the same face about Kevin. Aled didn't mind Kevin. Hell, they even got along relatively well, even though they had nothing in common outside of sex and who they liked to do it with. Aled certainly trusted Kevin to look after Gabriel and he didn't stay up worrying or getting mad when Gabriel went round there.

It was just Michael.

It *had* to be just Michael.

His urge to stake a bit of a claim — especially after Gabriel's reluctant agreement — was still strong on Friday, though, so he texted at lunchtime, asking after the possibility of thieving Gabriel for the weekend.

Okay :) came the reply. *But be gentle at least tonight. Just done my T shot.*

Aled smirked. Gentle, sure. Possessive and dominant could be gentle too.

He clocked out a bit later than he would have liked but headed straight up to Belle Isle, deciding to collect Gabriel from the flat — the possibility of a blackmail scenario was lurking at the back of his mind — and stop off on the way back to pick up a takeaway.

Only when he got to the flats, there was a battered Clio in Gabriel's never-used parking spot and voices in the stairwell.

"He can take his fucking opinion and shove it!"

Aled frowned, catching the communal door to close it quietly, and craned his neck to peer up the stairwell. He couldn't see anything, but the shouting sounded like it was coming from Gabriel's floor. And while the flats weren't the nicest place in the world, Aled had never arrived to see blazing rows taking place on the landings. Heard them from inside other flats, sure, but not right out on the landing.

"That's fucking bullshit! Does he fucking pay you or something?"

There was a frosty reply, a little too low to be made out, but Aled knew the rhythm of the voice anyway. Gabriel. Which meant the shouter was probably —

Aled thinned his lips and took the stairs stealthily, fully intending to hear as much of this row as possible.

"No, I won't fucking clear off! Your new fuck doesn't control me, and neither do you!"

"This is my damn flat—if you don't sod off, I'll have the police out."

"Then fucking call them! I'm not fucking moving until you give me a damn good reason why—"

"Because I bloody said so—that's reason enough!"

There was a bang and Aled sprinted the last flight, to swing up onto Gabriel's landing and see both men squaring off. Aled had only seen Michael once before and hadn't noticed then how tall he was. He towered over Gabriel, one hand planted flat on the doorframe, the skin white with the pressure, and Gabriel scowled resolutely back, arms folded over his chest and not an inch of forgiveness in his stance.

"Am I interrupting?" Aled asked coldly.

Michael rounded on him—and for a split second Aled thought he was about to get decked. Then, with a frustrated noise through his teeth, Michael sneered and shouldered past him, pounding down the stairs as though they had personally insulted his manhood. Only when the communal door slammed did Aled let out his breath and loosen his stance.

Gabriel didn't move.

"Everything all right?" Aled asked warily.

Gabriel shrugged. He was frowning deeply, almost vibrating with tension.

"Michael didn't take well to being cut off."

"He sounded—"

"He's pissy as fuck."

Aled hesitated. He wanted to ask if Michael had actually touched Gabriel at all, but knew he'd get his head bitten off. So instead, he took Michael's place at the doorframe and reached out to rub his hands briskly up and down Gabriel's biceps, as though warming him.

"Okay?"

It worked. The tension leaked away and Gabriel pulled a face before looping an arm around Aled's neck and kissing him.

"Yeah. Just annoyed. He turned up about half an hour ago and started sounding off when I wouldn't let him in."

"You just dumped him on the doorstep?"

"I dumped him last night, actually."

"By text?"

"I called him. I'm not that crass."

Aled laughed, ducking to the side and nipping at Gabriel's earlobe. He still felt possessive but clamped down on it in favour of humour. Throwing his weight around right now wouldn't do any good for either of them, especially if Michael hadn't actually punched Gabriel or anything like that.

"I was hoping to steal you. Got an overnight bag ready?"

"Not quite. That knob interrupted."

Aled was allowed in while Gabriel finished packing a bag, though for once he didn't feel like accosting Gabriel the moment he could. Instead, he perched on the end of the bed and made idle conversation, trying to distract them both from Michael and his temper, and when the bag was zipped up, caught at Gabriel's wrist and pulled him down to the mattress for a hug.

"This isn't your place for the weekend," Gabriel complained, all elbows and knees as he squirmed around into a more comfortable position.

"In a bit," Aled said, squeezing tightly and nuzzling at Gabriel's hair. The bedhead was spectacularly impressive today. "Love you."

"Oh, God. What do you want."

"Nothing! God, you're so hard to compliment."

Gabriel laughed, trying to wriggle free, so Aled followed, latching on again and wrapping all his limbs around that lithe form, squashing Gabriel close and rattling off a series of enormously cheesy compliments, ranging from that bedhead to the fact his feet weren't cold when he put them on Aled's calves during the night.

Only when Gabriel finally gave up fighting and collapsed sniggering against Aled's chest did Aled consider the distraction a success and showered his face and hair with little kisses until Gabriel started to snuggle back and they ended up in a tangle of warmth and relaxation.

And Aled just didn't *want* to let go.

It took them an age to leave the flat. Aled felt possessive and affectionate all at once, and Gabriel didn't seem to be in any kind of mood to discourage him. But with Michael's presence lurking in the back of his mind, Aled didn't want to give in and stay at the flat either. So eventually he insisted — though they still didn't get home until after midnight. And judging by the hand that strayed to Aled's thigh somewhere around the A650 and stayed there all the way into Wakefield, the time did nothing to Gabriel's energy levels.

"You're getting cheeky," Aled warned as he pulled off the main road into the housing estate.

"Perhaps."

"I'd not, if I were you."

"Why?"

"You wanted gentle. Don't put me in the mood for teaching you a lesson if it's gentle you're after."

The hand was removed, albeit slowly and with trailing fingers, and Aled chuckled as he pulled up into the driveway and hauled on the handbrake.

"Get yourself inside," he said. "I'm going to put the car in the garage. And once you're inside, you're *staying* in there until Sunday night, so I suggest you don't leave anything in the car you'll be wanting later."

Gabriel's breath caught. Then he was gone, a shadow up the garden path, and Aled smirked. Gentle or not, this was going to be fun. And the bruise from the shot was always gone by the following day, so he didn't need to be soft for long.

He took his time, even pausing in the garden to check on the flowers, before letting himself into the conservatory. Gabriel had disappeared, his bag abandoned in the hall. A light had been switched on upstairs and Aled slowly shed his jacket and shoes before hooking the security chain across the front door and heading up to his bedroom.

"Stand up," he said casually as he entered, shutting the door behind him. He bolted it then slid a numeric padlock through the empty space to prevent the bolt being drawn back again. "If you want out of this room, you'll have to earn it."

Gabriel stood at the end of the bed, chewing on his lip. Aled teased it out with a thumb and tapped it.

"Stop biting that."

"Yes, sir."

"Good," he crooned, stroking Gabriel's neck before dropping his hands to Gabriel's jeans. He smacked

Gabriel's hands away when they tried to help. "Don't do anything until I tell you."

He stripped Gabriel efficiently of his jeans, underwear and socks, but left his tight T-shirt in place. Sometimes he was allowed to play with Gabriel's chest, and sometimes he wasn't. And unfortunately, he was yet to figure out a pattern to his permission. What Aled had in mind tonight wasn't entirely compatible with Gabriel's complicated feelings about his tits, and he didn't want the dysphoria turning up to ruin his plans — so the T-shirt stayed on, even if the gentle rise suggested Gabriel was wearing a bra instead of a binder.

It wasn't an impediment, though. Those narrow wrists were bound together with a silk ribbon, a deep and almost violent blue against Gabriel's pale complexion, and another roll of silk was rummaged up from the bedside drawers. Aled began to twist it in complicated patterns around Gabriel's torso, binding his arms to his chest so forcefully that he could barely even move his shoulders, the T-shirt flattening so tightly that every contour of muscle and the swells of his breasts could be seen through the cotton.

"You can play away all you want," Aled said conversationally as he knotted the silk behind Gabriel's neck and reached for another, shorter, piece of ribbon, "but this weekend, you belong to me. Your pleasure is incidental. If you behave yourself, there's no need for anything to hurt. But if you disobey me, then I will hurt you. And I take what I want anyway. Whether or not you like it is up to you. Are we clear?"

"Yes, sir."

Gabriel's voice was a breathy whisper and his eyes were cast downwards. Bound tight in the ribbon, naked from the waist down, he was the picture of submission.

Aled slipped the length over his eyes, that blackness vanishing from view, and secured it tightly. The picture complete, a shiver of uncertainty nevertheless vibrated in the back of Aled's mind. After a blazing row with Michael on the doorstep, Gabriel was now here, promised violence if he resisted —

He cupped that narrow face in both hands and gently kissed Gabriel's lower lip. Chaste. Sweet. Barely even there.

"Colour?" he whispered.

Gabriel's reply was immediate. "Green."

Aled nudged their noses together for a brief moment, just to feel Gabriel breathe, then pulled back and steered him onto the bed. He didn't say a word, merely arranged Gabriel as he pleased — face-up, caught between rows of pillows, pinned in place by softness and silk. Raising Gabriel's hips onto a cushion opened his thighs naturally and Aled spread them farther with his hands, before squeezing both knees.

"Stay there."

When he let go, Gabriel remained perfectly still. His cock was already thicker, his thighs pink with pooling arousal, and Aled stripped quickly before finding a bottle of massage oil that doubled up as lube and settling between those spread legs. They shivered at the first touch of Aled's slick fingers to Gabriel's already damp pussy.

"Don't move," he warned in a deceptively soft tone, stroking his fingers gently up the short, swelling shaft. "If you do, I'll get the wire to hold you still and rip bloody holes in your pretty legs while I fuck you."

The shiver vanished as quickly as it had appeared. "That's better."

He didn't say much as he worked Gabriel open with gentle fingers and persistence. Aled's instincts always defaulted to dirty talk and threats, but something felt wrong about doing so after the scene in the stairwell. So instead, he busied his mouth on soft skin stretched tight over slim hips, on the gentle swell of Gabriel's belly and the heave of his chest through sweat-soaked cotton as Aled worked.

And when his hand was buried to the wrist in Gabriel's slick heat and Aled flexed his fingers gently like an opening sunflower, he rose up to catch the cry between his lips and hold that precarious silence.

This weekend, Gabriel would be owned.

But it wouldn't be like all the other times.

* * * *

Aled leaned against the doorframe, cock in lubed hand, and smirked.

He'd left Gabriel in the spare room overnight — still trussed up tight in those ribbons, ankles tied with fresh ones to the bedposts and a gag added between his teeth to complete the picture.

It was tempting, given Aled's usual preferences, to wake Gabriel with a slap and start the day by turning him over and dry-fucking him for some imagined infraction. To humiliate him and make use of his body. To make him come, crying, on Aled's cock then fuck him again before he was ready.

But the memory of Michael's white-knuckled grip on the doorframe in the hall made such urges feel…disturbing.

So Aled moved silently to the end of the headboard, massaging his cock to hardness, and raked his gaze down that long, lithe form. The ribbons were twisted now, deep blue strings on white skin, and those freed thighs were cum-stained and bruised with bite marks. The faint sheen of lube could still be seen.

A mess. A bound and gagged mess that wouldn't be able to do anything but take every thrust into his tight, warm body.

Aled dropped onto the end of the bed without warning.

Gabriel stiffened, his knees drawing up a little towards his hips before his ankles could be pulled no farther. The tension was sudden and palpable, but although the hands bound tight under his jaw were curled into fists, the thumbs were on the outside. Visible. His mute green for when his mouth was busy.

God, he was so fucking *beautiful*.

Aled pulled.

In a smooth rush over the mattress, he dragged Gabriel down onto his slick cock. Despite the fresh coat of lube, Aled's skin still caught on the sticky mess from the night before, then punched through to the tight, silken grip beyond. Gabriel yelled around the silk, his thighs pushing weakly as though trying to pull away, but Aled slid his hands down to silk-bound hips and held him fast.

Then, without a word, began to thrust.

It was indescribable. Aled fucked in short, sharp movements, making Gabriel's entire body rock with the motion. His skin strained at the ribbons but couldn't break free. He wriggled and wrenched at Aled's grip with every withdrawal, only to shudder and gasp with every thrust back inside. As Aled's grip on those narrow hips tightened to the point of bruising, Gabriel's teeth ground down on the ribbon until it frayed and gave way.

The gasp—the high, reedy gasp, punctuated by Aled's thrusts until it turned into a panting whine—was shockingly loud in the otherwise quiet room.

Aled clamped a hand roughly over Gabriel's mouth and silenced him. He moved up that trussed body, still fucking it so hard that the bed was shaking, and spread his weight across the ribbons. Their pattern rubbed into his skin in ridges until he fought to breathe and fuck at the same time. As everything began to narrow and the room darkened around the corners, Aled forced his arms under Gabriel's back and crushed him close, pinning him so that he could do nothing but be fucked open, plundered, destroyed, *ruined*—

When Aled came, it was terrifyingly sudden.

He left bruises, he was sure of it. For a long moment, all he knew was the slick grip on his dick and the ragged gasps under him. The catch of ribbon and the shivering body in his arms. Used. Soaked. Debauched and defiled.

Fucking beautiful.

Aled caught both hands in Gabriel's hair to kiss that gasping mouth, licking into it and swallowing the noise. Gabriel whined and tried to pull away, but Aled took what he wanted regardless then finally pulled his soft cock out in a slippery rush and climbed off the bed.

"Please—" Gabriel whimpered.

Aled ignored him, opening the bedside drawers and retrieving a few toys. He was careless, turning Gabriel over by the hips without a word to slick up a plug and bury it in his arse, too hard and too big, ignoring the cry and the breathless plea for it to be removed. A new gag found its way between those teeth, silencing the desperation, and Aled took his time teasing pink lips out around the ball. The silk at his ankles was cut away with scissors and replaced with more ribbons to bind his feet together, leaving only his knees free.

Aled parted them with firm hands, ignoring the twitch in his dick when Gabriel squirmed and tried to pull away, and pushed a vibrator into the space he'd left behind.

And switched it on.

Gabriel *howled*.

His back arched powerfully, the ribbons straining against the jolt, and Aled had to hold him down with a firm hand on his belly, the other fucking him almost casually with the vibrator. Gabriel's skin was slippery with sweat and he yelled as Aled rubbed a thumb over his shaft with every thrust — then his knees and thighs twisted together, ground tight around Aled's wrist and he came shuddering and twitching like a butterfly on a pin.

He looked exhausted. His skin was flushed, fingerprint bruises mottling the pink to purple where Aled had held him down. The ribbon was near-black, damp with sweat and lube and cum. His nipples were peaks through the wet cotton of his T-shirt and Aled idly rubbed his thumb over one before seizing Gabriel by the shoulders and hauling him roughly off the bed and over Aled's shoulder. Gabriel hung limply, whimpering around the gag, and Aled smirked as he carefully carried him downstairs, rubbing a hand teasingly over that bare, exposed arse. The silence would be as torturous as the ribbons, he knew. Gabriel wouldn't know what Aled had in mind or what was going to happen next — and that would be as bad as whatever physical punishments Aled could come up with.

So he still said nothing, dumping Gabriel unceremoniously on the carpet and arranging him over the coffee table like an ornament. Zip ties, this time. Harsher on the skin and less forgiving than ribbon. He was strung face-down, tied to the table top by the neck, shoulders and waist then both thighs lashed to the wrought-iron table legs. Leaving that pretty backside perfectly exposed and Gabriel completely and utterly immobilised.

And Aled was a patient man.

He stroked Gabriel's thumbs one by one, barely visible under his neck, silently checking the colour, then — when they stayed exposed — walked away.

Just walked away.

And *stayed* away.

He was well-suited to torturing submissives via time. When he'd first started playing in his late teens, it had been a lot harder — mostly because his dick could get a lot harder a lot quicker. But Aled was going to be thirty-six in a few weeks and time was taking its toll. He wouldn't be ready to fuck again for a little while.

And that had made him patient.

Very patient.

After breakfast — which he ate with his feet up on Gabriel's back, watching the news — he put headphones over Gabriel's ears, simply playing him rain noises so loud that he would be rendered effectively deaf to Aled walking around the house, and left him in that sensory limbo. Unable to move, unable to see and unable to hear. And the result? Gabriel's sense of touch would go — did go — into overdrive.

Aled yielded to temptation midway through the morning, reaching between those bound thighs and massaging Gabriel to climax with just finger and thumb. It was possibly the fastest Gabriel had ever gotten off and he cried when Aled removed his hand and walked away again, straining against the zip ties until tiny lines of blood beaded along their edges.

Aled opened up that pretty little arse around lunchtime, with a liberal amount of lube and a ribbed dildo that had Gabriel screaming around the gag — and just as he began to clench and the zip ties twitched around his attempts to rut the table, Aled removed the rubber cock and left him again, open, empty and sobbing.

When he did eventually fuck it — as a reward to himself for finally cleaning out the fridge — Aled braced both hands on the coffee table and refused to allow an inch of skin to touch aside from his cock buried balls-deep and the crash of his hips into Gabriel's arse with every thrust. Gabriel begged and pleaded, clear as day even around the rubber between his teeth, but Aled was unmerciful. When he came, he didn't even replace himself with another plug.

He yielded enough as the evening drew in to remove the headphones and allow Gabriel to hear his place in the house, although he still said nothing and sat in their cuddle chair on the other side of the room, typing on his laptop. Gabriel's head twisted towards him and he occasionally tried to call out or cry, but after an hour of non-response, he seemed to sag and lie limply in his bonds again.

And Aled wasn't sure what to do next.

His usual ending would be to tear Gabriel free and fuck him as brutally as possible on the kitchen or conservatory floors—hard surfaces, hold him down until the bruises turned black, force him to beg for the fuck and call him a whore when he did. They would both come so hard that they'd black out for a moment or two, then Aled could ramp up the aftercare and reward Gabriel with all the attention he could muster for playing so beautifully well.

But that white hand on the flat doorframe hadn't dissipated.

To make it worse, Aled had seen the messages. Gabriel's phone had been singing in the kitchen most of the day and Aled had looked at the messages. Amongst the usual—Kevin sending funny memes, strangers on Grindr asking if he sucked cock, his neighbour complaining about the bloke on the ground floor—were nearly thirty-five texts from Michael. All sent today.

And they were—

Michael: I'm just looking out for you, angel.

Michael: Can't you see this is him trying to pull that abuser shit on you?

Michael: It's bullshit.

Michael: You need to call me.

Michael: Call me, angel.

Michael: Are you out with him?

Michael: You're not answering your door. I'll keep coming round until we sort this out, angel.

Michael: Call me.

Michael: I don't make demands on you like this, what's he got to do it? Dump him.

Michael: Last Friday was amazing, you want to give up last Friday for some jealous ginger cunt?

Michael: I'm not having this, angel, this is bullshit.

They were both aggressive and weirdly manipulative. Trying to plant ideas in Gabriel's head, almost.

And after reading the mixture of abuse, aggression and coercive reasoning, Aled felt oddly uneasy about doing anything that might play into Michael's hands. Doing anything that might make Gabriel second-guess his intentions — even if he *had* done those things under a verbal and physical green light.

So as the evening drew in, he decided instead to skip further punishment and head right for the reward.

He didn't say anything as he pulled the vibrator roughly free and ignored the temptation to smear his fingers into the mess and rub it into cool skin. Gabriel whimpered, muscles bunching, but Aled ignored that, too. He retrieved the scissors and began to cut away the zip ties. Gabriel lay still, although tense, as they were peeled away. He whined when Aled ran the blade of the scissors up his back and began to shiver when he was hauled back on his knees and the T-shirt deftly stripped off. The ribbon around his ankles was hacked free in rough strokes and Aled hauled at those bruised, stiff shoulders and dragged Gabriel up onto the sofa.

Then he removed the gag and kissed the mouth behind it.

For a brief second, Gabriel lay entirely still beneath him. Then, as though a switch had been tripped, he moved. Limbs clamped down. His legs hooked over Aled's calves. His arms came up around Aled's shoulders, one hand fisting in his hair. He clutched with fingers and knees and teeth, scratching when Aled broke the kiss, begging a simple and unclear *no-no-no-no* when Aled planted a hand on his chest and forced him down into the cushions.

Then he twitched the blindfold free and caught that face in both hands.

"Colour?"

Gabriel stilled. His eyes were wide and bloodshot. His fingers still clutched at Aled's shoulders. But he froze, like a deer in the headlights.

"Green."

Aled nodded, satisfied. "You're mine."

Gabriel swallowed.

"What are you?" Aled prompted

"Yours."

The whisper was reed-thin. Barely audible.

"Say it again."

"Yours — *oh*!"

Gabriel arched, chest shuddering, and bit down on his lip so hard that blood bubbled over as Aled slowly pushed inside. In one long, relentless stroke, he pushed his way back into that tight heat and settled like he owned it.

"Again."

"Y — *yours*."

Aled withdrew and slammed home again. And Gabriel got the idea, clutching hard again and burying his mouth against Aled's ear.

"Yours," he whispered. "*Oh*, God. Yours. Yours. *Yours!*"

It was brutal. It was messy. It was all limbs and breathless voices, fingernails and blood and tight, wet, *maddening* heat. And when Gabriel lost the ability to form words and just yelled with every hit, Aled drew out entirely and flipped him over.

"No! No, please—!"

Aled held him down by the back of the neck and leaned in close.

"Say it."

"Please, I can't—*please*, hold me, please, please—"

"Why would I hold you?" Aled prompted softly.

"Because—because I'm yours. *Yours.*"

Aled rammed home. Gabriel yelled, but then his hands scrabbled at Aled's arms and when Aled dropped his weight, Gabriel simply pushed back into it, forcing Aled to hug him, to hold him, to crush him close.

"Yours," Gabriel stammered, even as he flinched from the resulting thrust. "Oh, God—yours, yours—*more*, please!—yours—"

A hand left Aled's wrist. He stopped it.

"That's mine, too," he whispered, pushing his fingers down into the crop of hair and finding wet, hot pleasure. Gabriel cried and clutched at his arms, the breathless pleading dissolving into mere vowels, until—

He came apart violently under Aled's weight. Shaking. Gasping. His chest heaved and Aled could do nothing but press his lips to an exposed ear and groan as the pressure brought him to completion, his heart skipping a beat at the ruined wreck of a man under him.

Then he shifted and the wreck moved.

"Stay."

Fingers closed tight around Aled's wrist.

"Please."

Gabriel's voice was destroyed, and Aled kissed his neck, his ear, his jaw, his cheek.

"Please stay."

Aled smoothed back sweat-soaked hair, kissed the very corner of his mouth — and stayed.

Chapter Eight

Gabriel blinked.

Dark. Warm. *Really* warm.

He turned over, burying his face in the heat. There was a drum beating nearby, but dulled, as though he was underwater. The softness around his back contracted. The murmur of voices, like the come and go of an idle tide, ceased.

"Hey."

The whisper brushed his ear, followed by fingers. Gabriel nudged his face into them and the drums were disguised under a gentle laugh. He blinked muzzily. Not drums. Heart. Heartbeat.

Aled's heartbeat.

His brain finally came back online. They were curled up in the cuddle chair. He was dressed in Aled's pyjama bottoms, and the TARDIS fleece was wrapped around the pair of them, but Gabriel didn't remember getting there.

He didn't remember anything after that final fuck.

And he didn't want to. It had been *amazing*. So he burrowed his face into Aled's neck and huffed.

"Okay?"

He hummed.

"Gabriel—"

An alarm bell went off in his head. Gabriel rummaged for thoughts. For *sense*. He knew that tone and it wasn't a good one. Why wasn't it a good one?

Oh.

He found some muscle strength and looped both arms around Aled's neck, clumsily kissed his ear and nuzzled his nose into the damp spot that his lips left behind.

"Was 'mazing."

A soft sigh was his only answer and Gabriel squeezed. He'd spaced. He knew it—could feel the haze around his thoughts, stronger than any drink he'd ever had—but he could also hear the slight edge in Aled's tone. Feel the hesitance in his touch.

Aled was worried he'd gone too far.

So Gabriel squeezed, burrowed blindly at the side of his face and tried to awkwardly project his contentment while his brain was still too foggy to string much more than a few words together at a time. Tried to push his own pleasure off to the side for five minutes, when it was the only thing he was capable of really processing.

"'Mazing," he repeated.

"Yeah, I got that, sweetheart. Anything—anything hurt?"

"Nope."

Well, almost. He felt a bit like he'd been fucked with a traffic bollard. Fucked hollow. But it was a good kind of fucked hollow, and every time he moved, a little burst of contentment radiated outwards, singing along his tired muscles and sinking into bone like the happiness wanted to be part of his DNA. It felt like sinking into a Jacuzzi after a long, hard workout. It felt like running a marathon – barefoot and unprepared – but then collapsing into a sauna with the world's fluffiest towel between him and the boards.

It felt like fucking paradise.

"K'p me."

"What?"

"Keep me."

Aled chuckled. "Keep you?"

"Mm. Christmas soon. Be a present."

"For you or for me?"

"Both."

A hand dipped below the fleece blanket and stroked his bare back. Gabriel hummed again, then shifted until he could sling his legs over Aled's lap.

"You okay?"

Aled ducked his face into Gabriel's elbow and kissed it. "I am now."

"Sure?"

"Yeah. This helps."

"I spaced. Twice."

Gabriel felt the relaxation sweep through Aled's upper body. Gabriel could be slow as hell after he'd spaced. And it was the slow that triggered Aled's worries the worst. The failure to respond quickly when the game was over. The failure to always recognise that the game was done and dusted. Aled wanted some instant reassurance – and sometimes, when he'd spaced, Gabriel felt like he was moving through treacle to give it.

"Was awesome, though."

"Good."

"Hungry."

Aled laughed quietly and patted Gabriel's knees. "All right, all right. Home cooking or takeaway?"

"What's in the freezer?"

"Probably some bolognese."

"That," Gabriel said, but hung on. "Um, who said you could leave?"

"Jesus, all *right*—"

It was all a ploy. If Gabriel was a demanding bitch, Aled's issues disappeared like water in a desert. And Gabriel knew that Aled knew it was a ploy, but the game was over so there was no master in the room anymore. He bitched until Aled slid an arm below his knees and lifted, then called him an old man when Aled breathlessly complained about his back.

"Call me that again and I'll drop you on the floor."

He wouldn't and they both knew it. And Gabriel put on a show, blowing in his ear and calling him decrepit until he was deposited—fleece blanket and all—on the kitchen counter.

"I'll cut you up and put you in the bolognese," Aled grumbled as he rummaged around for the boxes in the freezer.

"Okay, sure, get back to me with when that's *ever* going to happen."

He kept it up until Aled had got the spaghetti on and the boxes in the microwave to defrost, then lifted his arms and beckoned with wiggling fingers until Aled stepped between his knees and kissed him. Not gentle, not hard—just kissed him. Like normal. Gabriel smiled into it and slid his fingers through Aled's red hair until it stood up in spikes.

"Better?"

"Better," Aled agreed. "Thank you."

"Welcome."

"After dinner, will you let me get the first-aid kit out?"

Gabriel blinked. "Why?"

"You don't feel it yet because you're still riding the high, but your back is a mess."

"Is it?"

"Yep. Zip ties have cut you up."

Gabriel rolled his eyes but agreed at the withering look he was given. He retaliated by locking his ankles behind Aled's bum and making him stay within the V of Gabriel's thighs and stir the spaghetti by reaching over with the spoon.

"You're clingy," Aled commented.

"And you need clingy," Gabriel replied.

"Clingy and bitchy."

"And I'm being both. Case closed."

Aled chuckled, quickly kissing the side of his head. "Yeah, yeah. Love you too."

Gabriel's stomach curled warmly inside him and he relaxed into Aled's shoulder, rocking them lightly. A sleepy contentment was warring with the hunger.

"You okay?" Aled murmured.

"Tired."

"No surprises there. Get a meal down you, then crash out. I'll let you sleep in tomorrow."

"Let me? Join me, more like."

"I have a couple of errands to —"

Gabriel pinched.

"Ow! Fine, fine. I'll do them Sunday."

"Better."

Aled smirked then softened. He set the spoon aside, turned the burner down until the pan was simmering gently, then rested both hands on Gabriel's knees.

"Need to talk about any of it?"

"No. Do you?"

He laughed gently, ducking his head. "Not anymore."

"It wasn't like your usual stuff," Gabriel admitted, hooking his hands around the back of Aled's neck and toying with his hair. It needed cutting. "You're usually a bit more brutal. And faster."

"Fancied a change," Aled said.

"Really?"

"Yep."

He smelled a rat.

"Aled—"

"I saw some of the text messages Michael's been sending," Aled said carefully. "And after the row you were having on the landing, it didn't feel right to smack you around and threaten you. So I tried a different approach. And it worked."

"You're telling me it worked—"

Aled chuckled, smoothing his hands up Gabriel's sides. It stung vaguely and Gabriel figured that Aled wasn't wrong about his back.

"You got very clingy."

"I did? When?"

"After," Aled said.

"Oh. I spaced."

"Yeah, I noticed."

"Was—exciting, but scary."

"How do you mean?"

Gabriel took a breath. He'd been hoping not to raise this part, but honesty was the best policy. He'd just have to word it carefully, so as not to set off any of Aled's issues. "If—if we'd not been in the house, I'd not have let you do it."

"Oh?"

"I couldn't always tell it was you."

Aled blinked.

"I know it's in our agreement that you don't make me sleep with other men, and I think because we were here, I didn't question that it *had* to be you. But if we'd been somewhere else, like a hotel room or a BDSM club or something, I might have questioned that and stopped it."

Aled licked his lips. Gabriel stretched up to kiss them, but there wasn't much response.

"I wouldn't have," Aled said quietly. "That's—you know that's why I've never taken you to a club."

"I know." Gabriel stroked his hands, still planted on Gabriel's waist. "But you know what it's like. I *know*, but I might have doubted it anyway. Just for a second. If we weren't here."

Aled nodded, but the shadow passed when Gabriel kissed him again. He responded, stroking a finger over the shell of Gabriel's ear and down his jaw before stepping back and unlocking himself from Gabriel's legs.

"Hey! Come back."

"Food."

Gabriel grumbled, but then his stomach joined in, and he lost the battle for another countertop kiss. Spaghetti bolognese was produced, and a tray of snacks and sweets to go with it. Aled might have been the master, but Gabriel had trained him well—food, and lots of it, had to be produced after sex games. Any food. *All* food. And chocolate cake, peanuts, biscuits and spaghetti bolognese were a perfectly acceptable combination.

"If you stop cycling, you'll balloon in a week," Aled complained as they settled back down in the cuddle chair together, Gabriel taking up a spot in Aled's lap and digging in to Aled's bowl instead of his own.

"Good thing I like cycling."

"Weirdo."

"Excuse me, a whole *day* of fucking! How are *you* not starving?"

"A whole day of lying on various bits of furniture, you mean."

"With a vibrator in me!"

"It was mostly off."

"Bloody wasn't..."

Aled laughed and apologised by way of letting Gabriel have the whole plate of custard creams. Gabriel grudgingly accepted it but made his displeasure known by continuing to harvest Aled's dinner as well as his own. Despite carrying several extra pounds, Aled really didn't understand how to hoover his food. The man savoured. *Chewed*. Like sex, he took his time when sometimes it was a good hard gangbang that was required.

But at least he understood food comas. Once Gabriel's stomach had been stuffed into silence, he put the bowls on the floor and collapsed sideways into Aled's arms, turning over in them like a contented cat asking for a belly rub. And Aled's answer — which was the correct one — was to slide lower in the chair and heft Gabriel up to his chest.

"Hello," he said.

"Hi." Gabriel grinned. "Come here often?"

Aled snorted and patted Gabriel's crotch. "Usually here."

Gabriel pouted.

"And occasionally there, yes."

"Occasionally?!"

Aled squeezed him and craned down to kiss a patch of skin just below Gabriel's ribs. "You're ridiculous, you know that?"

"Ridiculous? Excuse me—"

"Ridiculously beautiful."

Gabriel groaned and batted at the side of Aled's head. The contented cat had had its fur stroked the wrong way.

"That was pure cheese."

"It was pure truth."

"Shut *up*."

Aled laughed, squeezing again. "Nope."

Gabriel squirmed to get away. Aled resisted and the tangle slid sideways until Gabriel wasn't sure which way was up and Aled's warm blue eyes were the centre of the universe.

"Love you," Aled murmured and kissed the bridge of Gabriel's nose.

"Prove it."

"Prove it?"

"Mhmm."

"All right," Aled said. "How?"

Gabriel grinned. "You could always leave *more* cuts."

"Yeah?"

"Mm. That was even better than my birthday."

Aled raised his eyebrows. "Wow. What brings that comparison on? You were swearing blind I'd shag you to death on your birthday."

"Yeah, but there's only so far I can space in an unfamiliar place."

Aled smiled, stroking Gabriel's exposed stomach. The heavy weight over the soft rise and fall of his belly, and the even softer downy hair covering it, felt hot and relaxing. Gabriel wanted Aled to put his head there and sleep forever.

"Make it more familiar."

Gabriel's smile widened. "Oh aye? And how am I supposed to do tha—"

"Move in with me."

Gabriel's brain stopped.

Boom.

Done.

Followed by the longest silence that the world had ever known.

Chapter Nine

"I fucked up."

Conversation from work to swimming had been all about the new head of accounting, and it was only when Suze emerged from the ladies' changing rooms already chugging a protein shake that Aled decided to bring it up.

Or, rather, blurt it out. Like he had on Saturday night.

"Why, someone catch you gawping at their junk in the changing room?"

"I asked Gabriel to move in with me."

Suze blinked and lowered her bottle.

"Why is that fuc—"

"Because I did it after persuading him to get shot of another regular and *right* after fucking him stupid all day."

Suze groaned. "Oh, God."

Yeah, that was the about the sum of it. After all that preparation, all the intention, all the planning it out— he'd just blurted it out like an idiot. Like a bloody teenager on a first date. Just word-vomited it out there like a complete moron and had gotten exactly the response he'd predicted.

"You asked a guy who was probably wary of his own mum to move in with you, right after sex?"

"Yeah."

"And a guy who's skittish about you because he's worried about possessive dominants going all jealous on his arse, right after talking him into dumping the other guy?"

"Yeah."

"What did he do?"

Panicked. Well, not quite panic-panicked, but—

"Went a bit white, stammered he'd think about it, then asked to go home."

Suze's face screwed up. "Oh, *Christ*."

"Yeah."

Suze sighed. Her hand locked around his wrist and she towed him to the cafe. The cafe itself was closed, but the sofas were available and Aled dropped into one of them with a heavy sigh. He felt hollowed out and exhausted. The initial gut-wrenching horror of the mistake had been washed away by exhaustion. He felt *sixty*-four, not thirty-four.

"Did you speak to him Sunday?"

"Texted him a bit. Apologised for just blurting it out and he said it was fine, but otherwise not really."

"Go round and talk to him properly."

"And say what? I can't take it back. I don't *want* to take it back."

To his surprise, Suze agreed with him.

"What?"

"I think now you've said it, you're better off repeating it."

Repeating it? Why the hell would he *repeat* such a stupid mistake? He'd be lucky if he was allowed to keep the keys to the flat now.

"Why?"

"Because otherwise, it really does look like you only said it because he shags good."

Aled frowned.

"If you repeat it in the cold light of day, with all your clothes on and no sex-happy hormones clouding your judgement, you'll be able to let him know you mean it."

"What's the point of me meaning it, if he locks it all up with getting rid of Michael and—"

"Well, that's what you have to do now."

"Make him believe it's not about making him mine and mine alone?"

"Yeah."

"How?" Aled implored desperately. "Christ, Suze, I've been with him almost two years and he's *still* afraid of me."

It bubbled up and out. Skittish was one thing, but— but what did it say? What did it say about Aled that Gabriel was still so wary of him after all this time? What did Aled expect? He beat him up and smacked him around and—

"Stop it!"

He scowled at his best friend and she scowled right back.

"He's not afraid of *you*," Suze said sharply. "He's afraid of a possible scenario. He's afraid of a theory. And—God, Aled, I hate to say it, but it's probably because he's trans."

"What?"

"He's got much more reason than most to default to this assumption that people are going to hurt him."

Aled opened his mouth—and slowly closed it again.

She was right—and even more right than she thought she was. Aled didn't know much about where Gabriel had come from, but being queer had a lot to do with the missing pieces. There weren't exactly loving, supportive parents waiting in the wings. It wasn't entirely the conquered alcoholism that made Kevin insist on staying in touch. It wasn't for courtesy's sake that Gabriel would text Aled screenshots of the accounts chatting him up on Grindr.

"I can't imagine being in his shoes," Suze said quietly. "I mean, it's always on the news, isn't it? About trans people being murdered when they get found out and stuff like that. No wonder he's wary of giving someone—*anyone*—a hold over him."

"Even me."

"It's not about you."

"Isn't it?"

"No." Her voice was firm. "No way does he not trust you. But you're asking for a totally different kind of trust. Even if—look, if you went nuts during a scene and hurt him or ignored his safewords, it will be over eventually and he can get away. But abuse isn't like that. It's slow and coercive and suddenly one morning you realise that's where you are and you don't know how you got there and you don't know how to get out. You're asking him to trust you now *and* in the future. You're asking him to rely on you being what he thinks you are in the long term, when there's no possible way he can guarantee you're *always* going to be what he thinks you are."

"But that's the same for everyone. You and Tom have to do that. Melissa had to do that."

"Yeah, it is."

"So what do I—"

"You're going to have to persuade him to make the leap."

"How?"

"Well, start with meaning it. He might try to handwave it as you being all fucked-out and happy and you didn't mean it. Mean it. Then—I don't know, maybe you need to hit the issue head-on instead of dancing around it. Maybe you need to change your games for a bit so he feels safer, or set out rules for *when* he brings other men home, make it clear you know he will do and you're okay with that."

Aled squirmed. Right there was the other problem. The one that had never come up with Gabriel, because they'd never tried living together before.

"I'm—not."

"Eh?"

"I don't like other men in my house."

"Oh, Christ, yeah, you went nuts after Melissa had that guy in your bed…"

"Well, it was my bed!"

Suze sniggered, then schooled her expression and shook her head. "Then figure out a plan. Maybe if you're not home, it'd be better? Like when you drink, you stay at mine? Or you could arrange a familiar hotel, agree to pick him up afterwards or whatever? But maybe if you do something to show you *know* there'll be other men in the future and you're okay with that, maybe he'll not be so wary."

Aled chewed on his lip, pondering. "Somewhere neutral," he decided.

"What?"

"I need to repeat it somewhere — neutral. Where he can't think I'm pressuring him. If I just go up to his flat and loom in his space, he'll close off even more."

"Oh, yeah, good idea."

"But if I take him out on a *date*, that could be even wor — "

His phone interrupted him, suddenly ringing shrilly in his pocket, and he groaned.

"God, that's probably work. That fucking new intern fucked up the Henderson account and you know what his lawyer's li — oh, shit, it's not."

It was worse than the weasel lawyer. Gabriel's picture was beaming up at him, and Aled swiped into the call with worry already flooding his chest. They always texted. Gabriel very rarely *rang* him. "Everything all right, sweetheart?" was Aled's greeting.

"Um, hello."

Aled laughed. "Sorry. Hello. You just don't usually call."

"No, well — are you busy?"

"Just leaving the gym. What's up?"

"Could you come and pick me up from work? I get off in half an hour."

Aled clutched at the reprieve. He wanted a lift. It was — normal. Just them stuff. He hadn't *completely* trashed things.

"Course I can. Anything in mind?"

"Dunno. Takeaway and a movie? Nothing special."

"Nothing special it is," Aled said and blew upwards into his hair when Gabriel hung up. "Okay, apparently it's dinner and a movie at the flat."

"Well, try talking about it anyway?" Suze prompted. "I think the longer you leave it, the less he'll think it's about you just loving him to bits and more about you wanting to control him. Especially if you don't mention it again until another shag, or another...other man." She then pulled a face at her phrasing.

"Yeah. Well. We'll see."

"Hey, if it doesn't work, you just need to keep at it and loving him and eventually he'll figure out on his own that it's just bad timing and your lack of brain-to-mouth filter."

"Excuse me, I filter far better than you do."

"*Sorry*?"

* * * *

"Sorry."

Aled blinked. "What?"

Gabriel, still leaning in his open window, pulled a face. "For bolting Saturday night. I'm sorry."

"Oh," Aled said awkwardly. "Well, that's all right. I shouldn't have just blurted it out like that."

"And for making you come up here to pick me up."

"That's fine. Hop in. I get a nice evening in with y—"

"It's just...Michael's been sending some pretty shitty things."

Gabriel's gaze dropped, and Aled's gut tightened.

"Like what?"

"Just—stuff."

"Like *what*?"

"Well, the one he sent before I called you was that he's not going to let the best shag he's ever had fuck off with some dickless ginger twat and who am I kidding by pretending I could ever give up being a slag."

"*What!*"

Gabriel shrugged. "And he was hanging around the building at lunchtime and tried to talk to me, so..."

He trailed off, chewing on the edge of his thumbnail.

"Right," Aled said tightly. "Christ, what a dickhead."

"I just didn't want to really be walking home on my own if—"

"Good," Aled said, reaching out to squeeze Gabriel's elbow. "Come on, sweetheart, jump in and I'll drive you wherever you want to go."

"Beach in Barbados?"

"Erm, in *this* country."

That finally smoothed the anxious look away, and Gabriel climbed into the passenger seat and leaned over to kiss Aled's jaw.

"Thanks for coming up."

"If you'd mentioned why, I'd have been here sooner."

"We don't close for hours. I could have pulled a few extra hours."

"Good. Look, Gabe—"

"—riel."

"—I'm really not comfortable just leaving you in the flat on your own if that tosser is going to be hanging about and calling you a slag, so—look, you're totally welcome at home if you want to stay the night with me, or I could stay with you. I don't want to just push into your space but..."

"I did intend on persuading you to stay."

A hand slid over Aled's thigh and dipped between them. A flicker of arousal sparked at the heavy weight on his legs, and Aled cleared his throat heavily.

"Persuasion done, but, uh, first," Aled said, removing it and kissing the knuckles. "Dinner? Proper little sit-down job? I want to talk about Saturday night."

Gabriel frowned. "I said I'm sorry about bolting—"

"And I need to say I'm sorry for just spitting it out like that, and repeat the request."

"You—what?"

Aled squeezed Gabriel's hand. "I do want you to move in with me."

Gabriel's mouth worked silently.

"And it's not about Michael. It's not about other men. It's not about keeping tabs on you, or controlling you. It's not even about *you*."

Gabriel blinked owlishly, and Aled took a deep breath.

"It's about me, getting to come home every day to a house that I share with someone that I love. Cuddles in bed on Saturday mornings, and shared dinners, and evenings on the sofa. Photos on the wall. Just— someone *there*. And a home with that someone. And given that someone is you, that home needs you."

Gabriel's fingers twitched in Aled's.

"*I* need you. Because I love you. Everything else— every single little thing apart from you, me, same roof—can be negotiated."

And those fingers closed tight and squeezed.

Chapter Ten

Gabriel's chest hurt.

His heart hurt, his throat hurt, his ribs hurt—everything just *hurt*. Because the earnest look on Aled's face, the soft tone of his voice...

God, he meant every word of it, didn't he?

"You mean that."

It wasn't quite a question, but Aled rubbed his fingers and said, "Yes," anyway.

"You really mean it."

"Yes."

Gabriel wasn't used to being wanted, and he was even less used to people expressing it. He knew how Kevin felt, but he still got uncomfortable if he said anything. He'd known how Jim felt, but would rail against affectionate words. He liked physical affection all day long, but he had no idea what to do with words. There was something starker about them. Something more difficult to process.

More difficult to accept, even as he knew them to be true.

"I —"

A lump formed in Gabriel's throat, and he bit his lip.

"Are you really that surprised?"

Gabriel snorted. God, Aled could be dumb sometimes.

"Yes."

"Why?"

The question was very soft, almost hesitant. Gabriel swallowed, but couldn't find the words, and for a long moment, they simply sat in silence.

"You know I love you," Aled murmured eventually.

"I do," Gabriel mumbled. "But enough that you want me there all the time?"

"Well, not one hundred percent of it. I'd still like to visit the bathroom in peace."

Gabriel laughed. It cracked in the middle and he choked.

"Oh, hey, *Gabe*."

The hug was sudden and hard and Gabriel clutched at Aled's jacket blindly for a minute. Christ, where was it all coming from? Michael had been a prick, then he'd been so flustered by Aled asking and worried about what it meant, and now *this*? That soft little declaration and Aled holding his hand like they were getting married, and —

Why was he *crying*?

"Sorry," he mumbled. "M'sorry, I just —"

"S'alright."

"I just — nobody's ever wanted me to do this before."

Not really. Kevin had offered, when things had been really bad. He'd stayed with Grandpa and Uncle Chris, but they were family. Even Jim — they'd not lived together out of choice. They'd lived together because Jim had lost his job at the factory and Gabriel had a double bed and they'd been trying the exclusive thing. It hadn't been — it wasn't like this.

"What, move in?" Aled asked.

"Yeah."

"Yeah, well, we've established that you've dated some real idiots…"

Gabriel laughed wetly.

"None of your other regulars ever wanted you to?"

"Kevin did, but Judith draws the line at having her husband's other subs actually *living* there. That's it. Everyone else — "

Gabriel swallowed, and shut up. Everyone else had wanted something in return. They'd wanted Gabriel to move in and play *married*, full-on forsake-all-others.

"They wanted me to dump all my other guys."

"I don't."

Gabriel dared to breathe.

"I don't. I still want Michael out of the picture, especially now he's harassing you and calling you a slag, but that's it."

"That's it?"

"Yeah. We can negotiate how we deal with them if you move in, but you're absolutely beautiful and relaxed after you've played your games with Kevin, and you're all lit up and cheery after a good first date — I love those parts of you, too. I want you to be beautiful and lit up all the time, and whoever makes you do it is welcome to carry on."

Gabriel swallowed. He scrambled for some semblance of steel. He didn't want to be sweet-talked and coaxed. He wanted Aled to understand it. He wanted Aled to really, really mean it.

"You — you have to mean that. You *have* to."

Aled's hand was tight. "I do mean it."

Then reality crept in again, and Gabriel shook his head.

"Gabe—"

"I just—"

"*Please*."

"I *can't*."

"Why not?"

"I—"

"Explain it to me, sweetheart. I know you're wary, I know you don't want a jealous dominant on your hands who can control what you're doing all the time, but—"

"If I moved in with you," Gabriel said carefully, "then I could end up completely reliant on you. *Completely*."

"How? You have a job, you—"

"Not much longer."

And there it was. The fear rose up in Gabriel's throat like bile, and he had to swallow so as not to be sick. The rumours were only getting stronger about the shop. Everyone knew it was only a matter of time now. He could be unemployed. He could be back on the dole, and they'd move him into a council flat, and everyone would notice the men coming and going, and rumours would start, and he'd get *tranny paedo* written on his door again, and—

"Gabriel? Hey, *breathe*, sweetheart, it's all right—"

Aled's hand was suddenly firm on the back of Gabriel's neck, and he swallowed, pushing back against it.

"It's all right."

He breathed. The low tone. The aftercare voice. He closed his eyes, reached out in his mind for the familiar grip of his master's hand, and *breathed*.

"There you go," Aled murmured. "That's it."

"They're talking about closing the shop," Gabriel croaked. "I'm job-hunting, just in case. But if I lost my job and we were living together, I'd be *completely* reliant on you. And you could — Aled, I don't mean it to sound like you *would*, but—"

"But I *could*. And that's enough for you, isn't it?"

Gabriel closed his eyes and wanted to cry.

"Hey. *Hey*."

A hand squeezed his knee.

"Has that happened before?"

Gabriel shook his head but unglued his tongue. "Only because I saw it coming."

Like how he'd never been raped. Like how he'd never been killed or seriously injured. He'd been lucky and seen the danger coming. Jim had been fine—the man had been gooey from head to toe, and about as dangerous as a rabbit—but there'd been others, other hookups, even other regulars. Other guys who'd pushed for moving in and commitment and exclusivity, and Gabriel had known what they wanted. A pet. A permanent fuck toy. A dirty little secret shut away somewhere, sometimes just from the wife and kids and sometimes from the rest of the world. Others who'd wanted to put him in a box, a cage, a prison, and keep him there.

Whether he liked it or not.

No way out. No safewords. No ending.

One guy had even outright *said* it.

"Gabriel, look at me."

And even without them, that was the way it had been before. He could still hear the shrill shriek in the back of his mind, in the very dark recesses where he'd come from. *Not under my roof. Not when you eat off my table.*

You're my daughter, and as long as you're here, you'll do as you're told.

He remembered that life.

He'd always remember. There was nothing anyone could do—not Kevin, not Aled, not Jim—to drive that out. He'd been reliant once and it had been torture.

He was never going to be reliant again.

"Look at me, babe."

He refused. The knee was squeezed again, then Aled's arm was around his shoulders and warm air was ghosting over his ear. Heavy. Comforting. Gabriel relaxed, even as he didn't want to.

"I'm asking you to make a leap of faith for me," Aled murmured. "I'm asking you to trust that I'm not out to control you. I call you mine, but this car is mine too and other people ride in it. My house is mine, but I have people over."

"When you say they can come over."

"My wife was *my* wife, she was *mine*, but she slept with other men. I was *hers*, but I slept with other men and women."

Gabriel bit his lip. Melissa. She'd not been exclusive either, but—

"I don't know why you're so skittish," Aled said carefully. "And if it takes the rest of my life to prove to you that you don't need to be skittish of me, then I will do it. But I'm asking for a leap of faith here, Gabe, and *please*, I'm asking you to jump."

There was that please again. Gabriel took a shaky breath—and thought.

If he lost his job, he'd be unemployed and living in Aled's house. And Aled could use that any way he wanted. If he paid all Gabriel's bills, then what would Gabriel owe him in return? Gabriel wasn't thick—he'd had guys try to pay the bill at the restaurant before, to say he *had* to do what they wanted in bed. His neighbour in the old flat had tried to make Gabriel sleep with a group of his mates, in exchange for them not beating him up for being trans. It could happen. It *did* happen.

Then he pushed past the instinctive panic and breathed again.

But then, this was a man he'd brought to the very brink of an orgasm then safeworded, and he'd never gotten angry or finished off anyway. This was a man he'd tested, again and again, and who had never failed. This was a man who he trusted to tie him to coffee tables, to gag him, to fuck his face and call him a dirty whore, and yet never hurt him beyond his limits, always respect the safewords Gabriel had brought with him to the scene, and look after him when it was over.

A man stroking his knee in a car, after having driven from Wakefield to Leeds to collect him from work because his ex was being creepy. With no expectation of any reward for it.

God, this was *Aled*.

And Gabriel was being stupid.

"We need to negotiate," he whispered.

Aled's hand tightened. His voice was very carefully controlled. "Everything about how is up for negotiation. Told you. You, me, same roof."

"Would the — would the roof be in Wakefield?

"I'd prefer that."

"What about me getting to work?"

"You're not far from the bus station. And I can drive you up or pick you up when your hours line up to mine."

"Would it be your house?"

"In the immediate, I think so. Could always find a place of our own later, if you wanted."

"So where do I bring my other regulars?"

Aled paused. A sick fear unfurled in Gabriel's stomach.

"I have to be honest here, sweetheart, I'm not especially okay with other men in my house," Aled said slowly. "I wasn't with Melissa and I don't think I will be with you. I'm sorry. *But*," he added sharply, "that doesn't mean you can't have them. Melissa sort of…pushed the issue too hard. I came home to find her shagging one of her workmates in our bed, and we'd not even talked about if we could bring our conquests home before. So I went a bit nuts, and I've stayed pretty turned off the idea."

"And now?"

"And now, I'm older and you're kinder than to just wave one of your other lads around in front of me, and maybe it won't be the issue it was then. I mean, not in our bed, definitely not. But it might be that I go out for the evening with Suze and I have a good time out with her and I'm not in the least bit concerned about coming home in the morning to find the spare bed's been made up new in my absence."

"What if you're not?"

"Okay with that?"

"Yeah."

"Then we'll figure out a workaround. Even if it's finding a nice hotel you can use regularly. I'm certainly not going to say you can't do it. And hell, maybe one or two of your regulars could come over. I've liked the odd time I've had to come to Kevin's to collect my new toy."

Gabriel smiled faintly, though it was a moot point. Kevin never played outside his own basement.

"We'll work something out. But it won't ever be a flat-out no. I won't ever try and say you just can't. I'm not trying to change your behaviour. Promise."

Oddly, it was Aled's mention of Kevin that let Gabriel relax. They liked each other — well, after Aled had freaked at some of the wounds Kevin had left behind and insisted on meeting him. Once they'd squared up and side-eyed each other a bit, then they'd gotten on well.

And if — if Aled was still okay with picking Gabriel up from Kevin's, both in and out of games, then maybe Gabriel *could* trust to fate with this bit?

Still...

"What about bills?"

"Well, I can afford them just fine, and you don't get paid much, but if it would make you too uncomfortable — "

"It would," Gabriel said flatly, and finally opened his eyes and glanced at Aled. That freckled face was calm and relaxed.

"Then we'll work out a way of dividing them up so you're not broke every month but you don't feel uncomfortable."

"You *can't* have a financial hold over me. I know I don't get paid much and I have, like, no savings, but it's still *mine* and — "

"And that's fine," Aled soothed, kissing his shoulder. "I want you to live with me and be your usual sunny, sarky self, not to live with me and feel on edge all the time. And you certainly don't owe me anything. Especially as I'm the one asking!"

Gabriel cracked a faint smile and scrunched his face when Aled kissed the edge of his mouth.

"Hey, let's go and get dinner and negotiate," Aled said softly. "And, tell you what, let's trial it first. You've stayed the weekend plenty of times, why not try staying a week? And after that, try staying a month? And if all goes well, and we're both liking it, you could move in proper?"

Gabriel licked his lips.

A week. He could do a week, easily. Maybe…maybe a bit longer? Get a *real* feel for it?

"Two weeks?"

Aled squeezed his hand and beamed.

"Deal."

And the smile was so wide, so brilliant, so *happy*, that Gabriel suddenly didn't feel so afraid.

Chapter Eleven

Aled left the flat the following morning, and it was intact.

He returned just after six in the evening, and it had been destroyed.

"What the hell happened?" he asked, standing in the open doorway, spare key still in hand, and staring at the clothes everywhere.

Gabriel, wearing nothing but a pair of jogging bottoms, shrugged. He folded himself up to sit amongst the melee again and returned to sifting through the piles.

"Deciding what to take," he mumbled.

Aled frowned slightly and hunkered down on the threadbare carpet to join him. "Hey," he said, squeezing Gabriel's knee. "Everything all right?"

"Not really," Gabriel admitted. "Michael was round earlier banging on the door and swearing at me. My boss texted to say I need to come in tomorrow for a big meeting about the future of the shop—i.e. I'll probably be imminently unemployed. And I decided if I'm going to lose my job, I might as well tone down on the stuff and figure out what I can sell on eBay."

"Sell your underwear on Grindr, you'll make a fortune," Aled quipped, then slid his arm around Gabriel's hips. "Well, there's nothing you can do about tomorrow, and Michael hasn't got the first idea where *I* live, so no more door-banging for a fortnight."

The smile was faint, and Gabriel's focus didn't shift from sorting the clothes. Aled grimaced. A bad day was one thing, but Gabriel wasn't in the habit of niggling and picking at his bad days. He usually threw a bit of a paddy, had a tantrum for half an hour then got back on track and cracked on.

This wasn't just a bad day.

"You're worrying about this, aren't you."

It wasn't really a question. Gabriel's shrug wasn't really an answer.

"Gabe—"

A flash of a frown.

"—riel," Aled added with a grin.

"I'm just tied up in knots between it's you and it'll be fun and fine and nothing's really going to change except I'll get squashed to death every night in my sleep, and—and it's a dominant who asked me to dump another regular and gets off on pretty extreme games."

Aled twitched but allowed the sting. "So do you," he said quietly.

"Yeah. Which brings me full circle to it's *you* and it'll be fine."

"Hate to say it, sweetheart, but there's no way I can prove to your skittish psyche that it'll be fine until you put yourself in that situation."

"I know."

Aled chewed on his lip, then tapped Gabriel's hip and hauled them both up from the floor. "Come on," he said, steering Gabriel to the sofa. "You're tired and tense, there's no rush to get home, and if you forget to pack something then we can always pop back and fetch it whenever you want."

"I'm not really in the mood for—"

"I don't always shove you onto sofas to shag you, sweetheart," Aled chided gently, pushing Gabriel to lie flat, then retreating to the other end of the sofa and perching on the arm. "Like I said, you're tense."

"So what are yo—ohhh, my God..."

Aled grinned. The press of his thumb to the underside of Gabriel's foot sent a visible ripple up that mostly bare body, and he drew both naked feet into his lap to massage them. He started with the toes—small, dainty things that gave bigger clues as to Gabriel's biological makeup than the vials of testosterone in the bathroom cabinet—and worked his way up, soothing high arches and hard ankles with soft sweeps and sharp stabs of his fingers and thumbs.

Gabriel relaxed fairly quickly, but Aled's true aim was to knock him out for a bit. Sleepy, he was pliant and contented. And Aled wanted both, not this twitchy, skittish man who had been wound tighter than a spring for days now. So even when the lines around Gabriel's eyes had faded, Aled kept working. Even after Gabriel sagged into the cushions and simply whimpered with every push, Aled kept going.

And only when those dark eyes slid closed and the stuttering rise and fall of his chest slowed and evened out, did Aled pause.

He waited, carefully stroking each delicate toe again, until he was sure that it had worked, then very carefully removed himself and tucked naked feet under a stray cushion to keep them warm.

"Love you," he murmured, stroking Gabriel's arm lightly before turning to the chaos. Right, as Suze would say. Time to wage war.

The heaps of clothes were relegated to a single heap in a corner of the room. Aled didn't think much of the idea of Gabriel selling his things to get by, so why worry about delaying the sorting process? He picked out some outfits for the coming fortnight — simple T-shirts and jeans, underwear that hopefully wouldn't be needed much, and made an attempt at matching socks before giving up and just finding twenty-eight individuals and saying to hell with it.

He ignored the kitchenette entirely, but the bathroom posed a new challenge. He was forced to nip down to the car for a couple of boxes and, after returning to eye the confusing mess of men's and women's toiletries, decided he was better off not questioning why Gabriel had five brands of moisturiser, and packed everything. The cloth bag containing Gabriel's testosterone prescription, ready for his next trip to the GP, went very carefully on top and was packed into the car first to be on the safe side.

He explored the bedroom more thoroughly than he had in two years, sure there would be some kind of treasured possession that Gabriel wouldn't be able to leave behind. But he found very little. There were no family photographs, no shoebox of memories stashed in a cupboard somewhere, no postcards stuck to the insides of doors. There was a computer hard drive, abandoned in the back of a wardrobe, and Aled rescued it just to be on the safe side, but suspected it had quite literally been forgotten.

Oddly, it felt — strange. He knew Gabriel had popped out of nowhere, so to speak, and that his origins were a touchy subject, but...really? Nothing?

Maybe Suze had been right. Maybe Gabriel was so wary for a damn good reason.

He stole the fleece blanket off the end of the bed, in case Gabriel wanted a home comfort, or they played and he needed it, and once he'd stacked up the few bags and boxes he'd corralled together by the door, retreated back to the sofa to remove the cushion and squeeze an ankle.

"Hey."

Nothing.

Aled huffed, grinning, and moved up the sofa. Kissing Gabriel's scalp got a murmur and a stir and he swiped both thumbs under bleary dark eyes when they flickered open.

"Hey," he repeated. "Come on. I've packed up a few things for you. We need to get cracking if we're going to have tea and get to bed at a reasonable hour."

"*Was* in bed..." Gabriel mumbled, then yawned widely. He lifted his arms and Aled ducked into the requested hug. The body in his hands was hot, smelling of sleep and serenity, and he tucked his face briefly into Gabriel's neck to kiss the plodding pulse in his jugular.

"I'm not carrying you downstairs, it'll put my back out," he complained, but squeezed a bit tighter before letting go. "Come on, beautiful thing. There's leftover lasagne at home if you fancy it."

The bribe worked. The foot massage and nap seemed to have worked, too — Gabriel was a bit brighter hefting the boxes downstairs and insisted on bringing his bike with him no matter how much Aled moaned about the idiocies of a bicycle when he had such a great car. The lighter mood was welcome, and Aled squeezed Gabriel's thigh as they set off and offered a takeaway and the scenic route.

As such, it was half-ten before they got home. And Aled caught the shift in mood the moment that it happened — as Gabriel put the final box down on the stairs, stood back, and folded his arms around himself.

"All right?" Aled asked, locking the front door.

"Mm."

"Gabriel?"

Gabriel blew upwards into his hair. "I just — I don't really know what to do now."

"Grab a shower and come to bed," Aled advised, tugging him close with a hand on his arse. "We've both got work in the morning."

"I've never just *come to bed* at yours. Come *in* it, yes. Not to it."

Aled rolled his eyes. "Well, now you can start."

"It just feels a bit awkward."

"Christ, you need domesticating. You've slept here plenty of times. You've showered here even more. Grab one, then the other. And if you're feeling a bit too twitchy and want to sleep in the spare room, then that's fine."

The casual offer seemed to dispel a little of the stuck feeling, because Gabriel kissed the corner of Aled's mouth and disappeared upstairs without a further word. Aled sighed, raking a hand through his hair. This was going to be a minefield. It'd be a miracle if he managed not to spook Gabriel at some point in the next fortnight. Maybe he really *would* need to make up the spare bed.

But still, maybe a fortnight off from Michael being a bellend would do wonders. Grimly, Aled remembered the first time he'd seen Michael, and ground his teeth. Shove-it-in-and-shoot, *really*. Fuck that.

He took his time, pottering around downstairs locking up and setting out his lunch for work the next day, before heading upstairs. The steamy bathroom had been vacated and Aled headed straight into it as though he was the only one around, brushing his teeth and taking one last piss for the night before rolling his shoulders, steeling himself and walking into the bedroom.

To find Gabriel sitting on the end of the bed, naked and looking completely lost.

"What's up?" Aled asked conversationally as he stripped off.

Gabriel chewed on his thumbnail. "Waiting."

"For me?"

"Mm."

"Didn't have to. You were pretty wiped out earlier, should have just crawled in and gone to sleep."

Gabriel shrugged a little. "Thought you might want to play a game first."

Aled's heart twitched, but he kept his expression neutral. "Not tonight. Too knackered, I'll be a zombie at work tomorrow." He climbed into bed and took off his glasses. The world blurred.

"You sure?" Warmth burrowed into the duvet beside him and fingers trailed down his chest. "You could just hold down and use me. Force me open. Make me pay for—"

Aled caught the hand. He twisted them around, catching Gabriel and turning him until they were squeezed together, locked chest-to-back. Aled's knees rose up behind Gabriel's and forced their bodies into spoons. He locked his arms around Gabriel's chest, catching both dangerous hands against their owner's body, and squeezed.

"*Stay*."

His voice growled and rumbled. It was his dominant voice, the dangerous one, and Gabriel went entirely still in his grasp.

"You are here for free," Aled said sharply, dragging his lips over the shell of Gabriel's ear. "You clearly need to be taught how to sleep with someone in the literal sense, so here's your order for the night. Stay still. Like this. Just like this. No sex. No scenes. Just you and me, *asleep*, until the morning. Got it?"

Gabriel's chest shivered.

"*Got it*?"

"Yes."

"Good." Aled squeezed and kissed the back of Gabriel's head. "Now go to sleep, you little monster."

Gabriel laughed shakily, then went quiet.

It took a long time before that warm body relaxed.

It took even longer before Aled actually slept. Instead, he lay awake for hours, clutching at something difficult to get hold of and hoping it never went away.

Chapter Twelve

Gabriel woke up alone.

Aled had a big bed, and it felt cavernous without him. Gabriel spread out in the sheets, stretching every muscle until his bones creaked, then relaxed with a yawn and opened his eyes to study the ceiling.

It felt — weird.

Nice, but weird. He'd stayed plenty of weekends, but longer stays tended to be in games. If he woke up alone in this house, it was usually locked in the cupboard in the spare room or chained to the spare bed.

Not free, in *this* bed, with Aled at work.

He had very vague memories of being kissed goodbye and hearing the car start on the driveway, but the insistent chirping of Gabriel's phone said it was nine o'clock and he needed to get up and go to work. Aled must have been gone for at least two hours. It felt odd to be here without him. And it felt odder still to throw back the covers and find his Tesco uniform hanging in the wardrobe.

Aled had obviously tidied a little—all Gabriel's clothes had been put away but his boxes were still sat in the hall. Too tired to bother unpacking, Gabriel borrowed Aled's toothbrush and deodorant, then let himself out and headed for the bus, still yawning.

The ice was lethal and he near-skated to the right stop. The bus itself was freezing and he huddled miserably in his jacket and hoped Grandpa would give him some money for Christmas. *Christ, Christmas.* It was only a week away. Would Aled expect him to stay? What did Aled do for Christmas? His nan lived in a care home in Pontefract, and Suze was practically his sister. He might have plans. Was Gabriel supposed to go to those plans? Gabriel usually went to see his uncles and his grandfather for Christmas, but—

His phone beeped in his pocket, interrupting his thoughts, and he groaned. It would be Michael. He really didn't want to deal with Michael right now.

To his surprise, it wasn't.

Kevin: Are you out?

Kevin had gone round to the flat?

Me: Staying at Aled's for a couple of weeks.

Kevin: Anything to do with the can of spam hanging around your flat?

Gabriel blinked. His brain was torn in two. Michael. And spam cans?

Me: Can of spam??

Kevin: I have the kids and Lily's learning to read. So mind your language.

Me: Ohhhh

Kevin: Was sitting on your landing and gave me a right earful for letting myself in.

Gabriel winced.

Me: If you'd called I would have told you I wasn't home.

Kevin: With that idiot hanging about, I wasn't going to be doing anything but checking in physically.

Me: Well I'm okay :)

Kevin: It's alright, I figured :) You always take your moisturisers when you go to Aled's.

Me: He doesn't use ANY, he's a complete MAN

Kevin: Neither do I. We're not all nancies.

Me: You might be happy to be badly groomed but I'm not.

Kevin: Watch it.

Gabriel smiled. For the first time since Michael had come around work yesterday, swearing and spitting, it felt natural. He felt — safe. Kevin was miles away, and Aled was at work, but he was safe. He quickly swiped out of the thread and opened his latest to Aled.

Me: Good morning :) I'm on my way to work. Are you going to pick me up later or should I ask Kevin?

Aled: What time you finishing?

"Bored at the office again?" Gabriel whispered. Morning commuters and old ladies didn't give a shit about people talking to themselves on the bus. And it would get him ready for four hours of smiling at his boss.

Me: Two. Only on a half-shift today.

Aled: Sorry I'm in a conference call two til four :(If Michael is hanging around, call Kevin.

Me: Will do :) Sorry about being so weird last night. Do you want me to get anything in for dinner?

Aled: Don't be :) Was thinking of making mince and dumplings?

Me: Never had those.

Aled: WHAT

Aled: That's not okay

Aled: Right we have to fix that

Aled: I'll be home by six. Get a packet of mince from work? At least 500g please

Me: Okay :)

Aled: xxxx

Gabriel smiled at the row of kisses and swiped back to Kevin. It was going to be fine. They'd have dinner and probably watch a bad TV show and maybe have some vanilla sex. Gabriel didn't really want a game just yet, not with the seismic shifts going on, but he wanted a cuddle and an orgasm. And Aled was pretty good at providing both, even if vanilla didn't get him going much.

Kevin: So what's the deal with the idiot?

Me: Michael

Kevin: Whatever. Spamcan.

Me: He's one of my regulars. I just dumped him. He's not taking it well.

Kevin: Prick.

Me: He keeps coming to work and hanging around my flat and saying Aled's abusing me.

Kevin: Is he?

Me: No!

Kevin: Then what's given Spamcan that impression?

Gabriel sighed, rolling his head back against the bus seat.

Me: Because Aled wanted me to dump him, and Michael said that's kind of creepy that Aled wants to control my boyfriend. And Aled wanted me to dump him because Michael treats me like a sex toy, which Aled thinks is kind of abusive and creepy too. So I can't win.

Kevin: Aled and I both do the sex toy thing too...

Me: Yeah but that's the only way Michael treats me.

He could picture the dramatic eyeroll.

Kevin: So why do you keep fucking him?

Me: I like it sometimes.

Kevin: You have two perfectly good guys who can do that for you without treating you like that all the time, you know.

Gabriel bit his lip.

That—that was the crux of it. He did. Now. But he hadn't once, and there had been Michael to scratch that itch. Back when—

He didn't like to remember it now, but back when Gabriel had figured it was as good as he was going to get. Back when he'd failed at his one and only serious relationship. Back when Kevin and Aled were mythological creatures found in fairy stories, not real men who really existed. Michael had been someone who wanted him, at least physically, and wanted to do him over and over again. He was someone who found Gabriel persistently attractive, and—more to point—Michael was gay. He had been the first gay man to want to fuck him, and Gabriel had been willing to overlook almost anything. Even now, he was the only gay

131

regular that Gabriel had. Aled was bisexual. Kevin was bisexual. But Michael was gay.

And it had meant something then.

Me: I know. Now.

Kevin: Do you?

Me: I'm getting there.

Kevin: So you dumped him?

Me: Yeah. He was making Aled uncomfortable and tbh he was starting to make me uncomfortable too.

Kevin: Good. You deserve better. You always have.

Gabriel swallowed thickly.

Me: You can't make me cry on my way to work, it's rude.

Kevin: Look at alllllllll the fucks I give!

Gabriel snorted.

Me: What about not swearing???

Kevin: They're busy colouring in the cat.

Me: You don't have a cat.

Kevin: I know but they found one...

He scrubbed the threat of tears away with the heel of his hand and launched the other bombshell.

Me: Aled asked me to move in with him.

Kevin: About time

Gabriel blinked.

Me: What??

Kevin: You're mad about him. He's good for you. He's a nice bloke. It's obviously serious, so it's about time.

Me: It's scary.

Kevin: Tell you a secret – it's even scarier for him.

Gabriel frowned.

Me: What?

Kevin: Having your sub move in is terrifying.

Me: That's not what I mean.

Kevin: ?

Me: This is the first time someone's wanted me to move in just because. Like…not because I'm a basketcase and need help or because they want to level up our sex games or because otherwise it's homelessness. It's the first time someone wants me around all the time just because and I've never had that before. Even my own mum didn't want that.

Kevin: Yeah well your family is another spamcan. Whole aisle of them.

Me: They done with the cat?

Kevin: Cat's done with them.

Kevin: Aled loves you. He was bound to ask eventually, with or without the Michael BS. Don't overthink it.

Me: What if it goes wrong?

His heart picked up. What if Aled turned out not to be the man Gabriel thought he was? What if they stopped loving each other? What if another regular — a *real* regular, like Kevin — came along? What then? What would they —

Kevin: Then it started off right.

Kevin: Don't go sabotaging it in your head without giving it a chance first.

Kevin: And you know you're not stuck.

Kevin: If it goes wrong, then you get out. You know we'd have you in a heartbeat.

Gabriel started to ask about Judith but was cut off before he could even send it.

Kevin: Me and Judith are talking about getting a bigger place now Gabby's arrived, and we were talking about somewhere with a flat or an annexe for you. It wouldn't upset her agoraphobia, but you'd be home where you belong.

The lump in Gabriel's throat came back.

Kevin: I think this will go right for you.

Kevin: I think Aled's will become home.

Kevin: I don't think it will go wrong.

Kevin: But if it does – IF – it's not your only home. He's not your only family.

Kevin: You already have one.

Gabriel swallowed thickly. A hot tear escaped and rolled down his face.

Me: YOU MADE ME CRY

Kevin: Hey, check it out! I still give no fucks! :D

Me: Son of an unmarried woman.

Kevin: While technically true, you've earned yourself a smacking for that.

Gabriel winced. Oops.

Kevin: You going back to Aled's tonight?

Me: Yeah, why?

Kevin: The spamcan.

Kevin: Don't worry about it.

Kevin: I'll sort him.

Gabriel blinked, and the tears evaporated.
Oh.
Well.

Me: So Michael may not be a problem anymore…

Aled: ?

Me: Kevin's going to sort him out.

Aled: …

Aled: OUCH.

Chapter Thirteen

Aled paused with the front door open and the key still in the lock.

"Gabriel!"

"Yeah?"

"What are you cooking?"

"Meatballs!"

Aled rolled his eyes and slammed the door. "Did you not fancy mince and dumplings then?"

Gabriel materialised halfway up the stairs, leaning over to peer down at Aled. He was towelling his hair dry and was dressed in a pair of boxers. The silent red, for when he didn't even want to be *asked* to play a game. Aled made a mental note and hung up his jacket.

"They're spicy cheese meatballs."

"If you say so," Aled said. "Want me to put some spaghetti on to go with them?"

"No, you have these with salad."

Aled screwed up his face. "*Salad*? Urgh."

Gabriel was visibly more relaxed than last night, despite the boxers. He cosied up for a cuddle, getting

Matthew J. Metzger

Aled's suit shirt damp. He smelled of lime shower gel and his neck was hot and tempting. Aled buried his nose there for a moment, then extracted himself when his cock took an interest in proceedings. Hugging Gabriel was dangerous at the best of times. Damp and naked was just asking for trouble.

"I want to talk," Gabriel said.

"Okay..."

"I want us to set out the new rules."

Aled blinked. "For—"

"For living together."

"I figured we'd wait until the two-week trial is done."

"I want to do it now. Or we're not having any sex for two weeks."

Aled laughed. "Okay, deal. But dinner first? I was held in a meeting through lunch so I'm starving."

"You dish up, I'll get the rulebook?"

"Deal."

Aled was surprised. He'd expected Gabriel to insist on either really violent games for the fortnight, or so-vanilla-it's-milk sex instead. He hadn't expected him to want to change their rulebook to fit the new situation, not given how skittish he'd been about the new situation even existing in the first place.

The rulebook appeared on the coffee table before they ate in the front of the TV, but it was ignored until dinner was over. The news was playing the latest scandal to rock Parliament. Gabriel was entirely uninterested in politics, which made watching the news with him hilarious—he was either laughably ignorant or spent the whole time criticising someone's hair. It was so relaxing that Aled almost wanted to waylay the discussion.

But then Gabriel took the empty plates into the kitchen, disappeared briefly upstairs and reappeared in his dressing gown.

Armour.

Made of cotton, but armour all the same.

He sat on the footstool instead of the sofa at Aled's hip and pulled the rulebook into his lap. It was nothing more or less than a small red book, filled with lined sheets and every rule written out in Aled's meticulous handwriting. He'd insisted on it, rather than Gabriel. Gabriel never wrote anything down, but Aled had wanted something tangible. Everything was in there. Their traffic light code on the first page — red for stop, yellow for pause, green for go. A list of banned terms on the second. Aled's own name, crossed out in violent blood-red as something never to be uttered in a scene under any circumstances. Details of a breathplay game that they'd tried once — and only once — which had driven Aled into a complete meltdown.

It creaked when Gabriel opened it, because the simple truth was that they didn't need it often. Their kinks by and large matched up, and they had both long since memorised the right and wrong language. It usually opened these days when they tried something new that didn't work and the last time had been in March.

But Gabriel flicked to the end and handed it over with a pen.

Carefully, Aled wrote a new title — *Rules for Living Together* — and set book and pen on his knee.

"Okay," he said. "Let's do this."

Gabriel breathed out and nodded. "Okay."

A slightly awkward silence descended. Aled fought back the urge to nervously smile. It felt oddly like they were starting all over again.

"You want to start?"

"Um. I don't — I have nothing that *permanently* needs to change, but — "

The fumbling eased Aled's nerves. Cool control settled over him. Dominants didn't dither. They made decisions. And if Gabriel couldn't get the words out, then Aled needed to step in.

"They're always up for renegotiation. And when you're all right for us to abandon a rule, just tell me. But what do you need, right now, to feel safe with me?"

Gabriel frowned. "I don't not feel safe with you."

"You're uneasy about this. That's not the same as safe. And I'm not blaming you for it, you can't help the way you feel. I just want to help ease you back down to safe, as soon as possible. So what rules would help with that?"

Aled kept his voice soft and patient, and watched Gabriel's fidgeting slowly ease until he finally said, "Money."

"Sorry?"

"You can't use money as a hold over me."

"Such as?" Aled prompted.

"Such as, you pay all the bills, so I owe you something. Such as, you're putting a roof over my head, so I should be opening my legs when you say so. Such as, you fund my lifestyle so you *own* my lifestyle."

"Ah," Aled said. "I get it. Okay."

He added it as the first bullet point, and the scratch of the pen on paper was soothing in the quiet room.

"Aled…"

"Mm?"

"Right now, I don't even think I can deal with you paying for dinner so I owe you sex."

It had been one of their early no-go rules, but swayed by some of the best scenes they'd ever played as they'd gotten used to each other. Now, it was almost an entry into a scene itself. If Aled insisted on paying and Gabriel didn't veto it with a safeword, then he would be taken home and subjected to some seriously hot play.

No more. Aled shrugged.

"All right. We'll put that on hold. Tell you what—if you feel comfortable with it, you tell me to pay and you'll do something in return. How's that?"

"Okay."

"Then we'll both know if it's safe. And I'll leave the living situation out of it entirely until you tell me otherwise."

Gabriel nodded, and blinked when Aled reached out to squeeze his ankle.

"What else?"

"No locking me in or out. It's—it's hard enough to think that I live here too. You can't control when I come or go."

Aled cocked his head. "What about punishment?"

During the summer, Gabriel had had most weekdays off while Aled was at work. And they had developed a game around it—Aled had punished him for an infraction by locking him in the flat and coming over twice a day to feed and fuck him. Like a housebound pet. It had been hot as hell and Aled had been entertaining the thought of doing it again in the New Year and maybe trying it out for a whole week instead of just a couple of days.

But Gabriel hesitated, and it was all the answer that Aled needed.

"I'll put it down—"

"Wait."

He paused.

"I like those punishments."

Aled waited, chewing on his lip uncertainly as Gabriel mulled it over.

"Maybe...maybe if you—if you didn't *leave* me there..."

"If I stayed in the house, you mean?"

"Yeah. And if—if I had a way out..."

"That defeats the point of locking you in," Aled pointed out.

"No, I mean, a way of—of safewording it."

"Ah," Aled said. He tapped his knee. "Well, we could use the bathroom, and put down a rule that if we're playing that, then I have to stay in the house with you. I could put the cord back on the safety alarm, so you could pull it if you wanted out."

"Okay," Gabriel said. "If you're home, and there's an alarm, then you can lock me in a room, but no other time. And you can't lock me out."

"I wouldn't lock you out of your own home," Aled said flatly as he wrote the amended rule down. "I might lock you *in*, but I'd never lock you *out*."

"I think—I think that's it."

"Okay," Aled said. "I've got one of my own that we need to talk about."

"What's that?"

"No men in my house that I don't agree to."

Gabriel frowned. "You can't control who I sleep with!"

"I'm not trying to," Aled said, equally sharply. "I'm saying I'm not comfortable with you bringing them home unless I'm involved somehow. It's—it might be something we can work towards together, but I can't be in a position where I come home and just find some guy fucking you in here."

Gabriel cocked his head. The flash of anger had subsided and he looked a little anxious.

"What happened?"

"Exactly that," Aled said. "I came home from work and found a stranger balls-deep in my wife."

He hadn't been expecting it. And at thirty-four, instead of the twenty-four he'd been at the time, Aled could rationalise it better. He'd been surprised, and that was the problem. He'd seen people he knew fuck his wife. He'd had threesomes with his wife. But to just come home and find it happening with a complete stranger…

He wasn't proud of his furious reaction, and it had become a rule on the back of the whole sorry affair.

"I might be all right if I'm forewarned, or I know the guy involved," he said. "But I don't know and I don't want us to just crash into that issue. So for the moment, no other men in my house. You can go round to theirs, or go to hotels—I will even pay for the hotel room if you'll let me, because it's safer—but I'm just not okay with other men in my house right now."

Gabriel chewed on his lip.

"Promise we can try and work it out better?" he said eventually.

"Yes. I promise."

"Then okay."

"Yeah?"

"Yeah. But you're not paying for my hotel rooms. That'll make me feel like you're renting me out to them," Gabriel added quickly and tapped the book. "Add that."

Aled made a faint noise of disgust. "All right. Agreed? No other men in my house unless I'm involved in the fuck somehow, but I won't pay for you to take them elsewhere."

"Agreed," Gabriel said, then tilted his head. Slowly, he crawled from the footstool onto the sofa and ended up straddling Aled's thigh. "What do you mean, unless you're involved in the fuck?"

Aled shrugged, his hand falling naturally into Gabriel's lower back. "You know, threesomes, voyeurism, that sort of thing."

"You want to?"

"Maybe. I like the videos your Kevin sends back with you. No different to being there."

"You'd want to watch someone fuck me, then have your turn?"

"Maybe," Aled repeated, and grinned. "You need to change the PIN on your phone. I've looked through several of your conquests."

"Yeah? Any catch your eye?"

"Not yet. I'll let you know if a likely one comes along."

Gabriel grinned and leaned down to kiss him. "Okay. But I get to choose them first. You can only pick in the scene, not in reality."

"Yeah, I know. Always your choice, you know that," Aled replied softly, then tapped his cheek sharply. "Stop changing the subject. We've got no using the financial situation, no locking you out, no other men in my house, and no paying for your hotel rooms. Anything else?"

Gabriel slowly sifted his fingers through Aled's hair and shook his head. "I don't think so."

Aled hummed and caught at his fingers, stilling them. "What about cameras?"

"Sorry?"

"Could I set up the cameras at home to watch you?"

Gabriel bit his lip. Aled simply waited. They'd talked about it once, but never done it. Aled knew that Kevin filmed Gabriel — in fact, Kevin's dungeon was covered in CCTV — but Gabriel's rules with Kevin were unlike his rules with anyone else, Aled included. Aled couldn't necessarily do what Kevin could.

Most of the time, he didn't want to.

But he quite like the idea of being able to watch Gabriel at home while Aled was away. Order him around via phone calls and text messages. Maybe get a little show on his lunch break. When they'd talked about it before, it had been vetoed not by Gabriel's feelings on the matter, but that it wasn't possible to hook up sufficient cameras in his flat without altering the plastering and pissing off his grumpy landlord.

Now, of course, *Aled* was the grumpy landlord.

But the circumstances had changed.

"I think I need *some* private space, at least at first," Gabriel said slowly. "But me and Kevin do that sometimes and it's *awesome*. So I don't want to say no."

Aled hummed. "Well, for now, we won't do anything. But in the future, what if I put them in the bedrooms, halls and kitchen, but I left you the living room, conservatory and bathroom?"

Gabriel mulled it over, chewing absently on his lip. Eventually, he nodded. "Okay."

"And I'll leave the cables exposed for a little bit so if you really don't like it and want them off, you can just pull the wire out of the back and deactivate it. Just text me if you do so I don't lose my shit at work and think something's happened, yeah?"

Gabriel chuckled and nosed at Aled's cheek before kissing him, their mouths askew.

"Yeah," he murmured messily against Aled's tongue. "That's it, I think."

"Okay." Aled smoothed both hands down Gabriel's back, ghosting gently over his backside before clasping at his thighs and dragging him — off and onto the cushions.

"Hey!"

"You're getting indecent in your boxers."

"I can take them off."

"If you want to go any further then you'll have to."

Gabriel laughed at him. The twitchy mood had eased and Aled was glad for it even as he was suspicious of the change from the anxiety last night. He sat back and raised his eyebrows imperiously as the book was removed to the coffee table and the boxers to the lampshade.

"And what exactly do you want me to do with that?" he asked when Gabriel planted his naked backside firmly on Aled's thigh.

Hands wound into his collar and began to pick at the buttons. A tongue played at his lips and a low whisper wound its way between his teeth.

"I want to ride your dick like it's what I'm built for."

Aled stretched both arms out along the back of the sofa. He was still in his suit trousers and shirt, and his cock wasn't even half-hard, despite Gabriel straddling his lap.

"Get on with it then," he snapped. "I haven't got all night."

The kiss was hungry. Desperate. *Wanting.*

But Aled heard the thanks and the trust behind it all the same.

Chapter Fourteen

Me: I need to fuck.

It was five minutes until the end of his shift and even the spotty manager didn't give a damn anymore. It was snowing out. Heavily. Gabriel knew full well he'd have to ring someone for a lift back to Aled's.

Aled: No change there then.

Me: No, seriously. I really need to fuck. Like a proper violent aggressive angry fuck.

Aled: Two things.

Aled: Firstly, I'm at work and while my dick appreciates the thought of smashing you up against a wall and fucking you blind, my colleagues probably don't.

Gabriel snorted with laughter and thumbed out half a text before he was interrupted.

Aled: And don't you dare tell me to wear looser trousers.

Aled: Secondly, I'm not ready for a brutal game.

Aled: I need to settle into living with you first.

Aled: Don't take this the wrong way, but you're still a bit too edgy for me to be comfortable playing one of our hard games.

Gabriel sighed and deleted what he'd been about to say.

Me: Called it.

Aled: Yeah?

Me: Mm. It's been vanilla sex for a week. I mean, I know you like fucking like snails occasionally but not every time.

Me: But you did say you'd step up to fill in Michael's gap.

He didn't want to push, but — the itch was getting too irritating to ignore. He'd always had a high sex drive, and the T didn't help matters much. Without Michael, and Aled screwing like a sloth lately, Gabriel was starting to shake right out of his own skin.

Aled: No Michael.

Me: No but I'm gonna ring Kevin.

He held his breath — then released it with a rush at Aled's immediate reply.

Aled: Okay :) Be safe x

Gabriel smiled goofily at the reply before clicking out of the thread. The twitch of anxiety settled and, without it, the throbbing in his work slacks got worse. He was going mad already. He only hoped Kevin wasn't watching the kids.

"Hello?"

"It's me."

Kevin snorted. "I know it's you. Not all of us have a contacts list that just says Grindr Fucks One through Three Hundred."

"It's not three hundred," Gabriel said defensively. "Anyway, are you busy today?"

"On my way home. Had a client."

"What kind of client?"

Gabriel could almost *hear* the eyeroll.

"The kind who wanted a new kitchen fitting, not a new arsehole."

"Any of the other kind tonight?"

"I have a feeling the answer is yes and it's you."

His voice was completely deadpan, and Gabriel fought the urge to laugh.

"If you're busy —"

"Shut up."

The hard edge had kicked in. Gabriel shut up. A little thrill chased up his spine.

"Are you at work?"

"Yes."

"Yes *what*."

Gabriel wanted a beating. He wanted it to hurt. He wanted to be fucked so hard he could feel it in his teeth and Kevin would need to call Aled to come and pick him up. Or to continue the game.

So he said nothing.

"I see." Kevin's voice—and Gabriel's dick—hardened. "What's your safewords?"

"Red, yellow, green."

"You're going to need them."

Then he hung up. Gabriel swallowed and dropped a shivering hand to his belt. He wanted to jack it—but Kevin wouldn't be far away. And Gabriel could run like a tap when he jacked off. Kevin would know he'd done it and if there was one punishment Gabriel *didn't* like, it was Kevin's punishment for wanking.

Cigarettes on his junk, no thanks.

He thumbed back into the texts and forced himself to stop shaking long enough to send his needs.

Me: I want you to beat me until I use my safewords to make you stop. Then you fuck me until I beg you to stop 'cause it hurts but then you do me anyway with something worse than your dick until I beg you to fuck me again. I want to be broken and you sell me to Aled 'cause he needs a new fucktoy.

It flowed out in a rush, and he sent a screenshot to Aled too. Kevin didn't reply. Aled just sent a thumbs-up. They'd talk behind the scenes. They always did.

"Liz! I'm off!" he shouted as he walked back out into the shop and picked up his jacket from where he'd left it on the back of his chair.

"You have another minute and a—"

"Blow me," he said and walked out.

It was freezing. His thin work jacket was no protection whatsoever, but his cock was burning like the surface of the sun in his briefs, and his arse and cunt already ached to be filled. They throbbed with every heartbeat, reminding him that they were empty and hadn't been really challenged in a week.

Kevin was going to rip him a new one. Maybe literally.

He went to wait by the side of the road and put his phone in his pocket to avoid temptation. Kevin had smashed them before when he'd caught Gabriel texting during a game, and Gabriel didn't have any money to buy a new one right now. So he stood in the deepening snow, hands in his pockets, and waited for the right car to slow down.

But the first one that did wasn't Kevin's old banger.

"Angel!"

Oh, shit.

That dentist advert smile beamed up at him. A hand patted the passenger seat.

"Get in."

"I'm waiting for someone," Gabriel said.

"It's great to see you again. Text your someone. Get in, let's have a catch-up."

"I can't."

Michael frowned, then the car dipped gently as the handbrake was applied.

"Come on —"

"I'm getting a lift any minute."

Gabriel's heart jumped as Michael opened the driver's door and got out. He was obscenely attractive in the snow, and he'd just come from the gym. Gabriel could see that sauerkraut of a dick outlined perfectly in a pair of extremely unforgiving shorts.

"It's not that black guy, is it?"

Gabriel raised his eyebrows. He stood his ground as Michael came to loom over him. He smelled of sweat and shower gel, with a liberal dose of Lynx body spray.

His hand was warm through the sleeve of Gabriel's jacket when he gripped his arm. A knee nudged Gabriel's thighs.

"I miss you."

Gabriel bit his lip and pulled back. The hand held on.

"Come over," Michael said. His grip was too tight. His other hand touched the small of Gabriel's back and drew him close. It was...claustrophobic. "It's been way too long. Like I said, I've missed you."

Gabriel could feel exactly what had missed him. He pushed back, but Michael didn't let go.

"I told you, we're over," he said. "You need to find someone else. I'm taken."

Michael snorted. "You've always been taken. Every man in Yorkshire's taken you."

The remark stung. Gabriel shoved and broke free. He paced a little way up the road, but Michael simply followed him. He caught at Gabriel's wrist and this time his grip was too strong to break.

"Fu—"

The horn cut him off. The anger rising in Gabriel's chest yielded to a wash of relief as Kevin's brakes squealed and the car door slammed. And Kevin *bellowed*.

Gabriel's insides shrivelled up in terror. Michael let go like he'd caught fire. A man on the side of the road stopped dead in his tracks. Lights came on in flats all along the street and doors opened.

Kevin might have said, "Get out of it." But in his ball-shrinkingly loud roar, it sounded more like, "*Gerradavit.*" An air horn of pure, unadulterated anger.

Gabriel dived for the car.

In a flash, he shot into Kevin's back seat and slammed the door, locking himself in. Out through the frosty window, he saw Michael hold his ground for all of four seconds before making the wise choice of turning tail. His brake lights came on then the road ahead was clear.

Gabriel let out a long, shaky breath.

The car dipped when Kevin got back in and he twisted around to peer at Gabriel.

"What happened?"

The master from the text messages was entirely absent. The frown wasn't anger. It was his friend. It was the man he had to stay in touch with. It was his family member who had said he'd sort it.

Gabriel rolled his eyes and said, "He was trying to get me to go to his flat."

"He was manhandling you."

"It hadn't got serious yet."

Kevin's tone said that he didn't care how serious it had gotten.

"Was he waiting?"

"No, just passing by."

Kevin hummed, eyeing him.

"I promise," Gabriel added. "He hasn't been hanging around since you said whatever you must have said to him."

"We didn't talk much."

Gabriel laughed. "You made a lot of noise and hit things?"

"I hit him. No use pussyfooting around," Kevin snapped, then nodded. "Fine. If he comes by again —"

"I'll call."

"Good."

"So —" Gabriel bit his lip. "Are we still playing?"

"Home and a brew first. Then we'll restart."

Gabriel nodded. He preferred the games to start with being picked up off the street, but the domestic punishment ones were good too. They'd have a cup of tea or coffee in the kitchen, then Gabriel would deliberately drop and break the cup.

Then Kevin would punish him.

They had a whole row of cheap Tesco mugs in their kitchen cupboards especially for shattering purposes. Sophie used them, Judith used them, Gabriel used them...but only for one thing. So they worked as a signal too, because when they got to Kevin's house, Judith was feeding the kids and gave Gabriel a knowing look when he took down the plain beige mug from the middle shelf.

He just smiled beatifically back at her and fished a teabag out of the box.

They talked for a while. He refused the offered food — he didn't like being sick, and Kevin's punishments would definitely make him sick if he ate — but gnawed on a couple of dry biscuits, watching and laughing at the exasperated parents attempting to place food in the children rather than all over the table, chairs, cutlery, crockery and tiles.

Then Judith hugged him, told Lily and Grace to give him goodnight kisses and hefted the baby up onto her shoulder.

"Let's leave Daddy and Gabriel to talk sports, shall we, ladies?"

"What sports?" Lily asked.

"Cricket," Kevin said, which was immediately decried as boring.

Gabriel said nothing, nursing his cup until the stampede had reached the upstairs bathroom and doors had safely closed between them and curious minds.

Then — very slowly — he stood up.

Took three steps to the sink.

And let go.

Almost in slow motion, he watched the beige ceramic spin towards the pale tiles. Brown tea formed a long arc in mid-air. His heart rose in his chest and pounded against his ribs as cup kissed floor, and the burst of cool adrenalin through his system was like being caught under the thundering power of the world's greatest waterfall.

Green.

Then Kevin hit him and the tile kissed his cheek.

Chapter Fifteen

The phone rang at nine.

It was late enough that Aled expected it to be the courtesy call from Kevin. The "He's staying the night with me." The "He's fine but we're not finished yet." The "Do you need a word before I cage him for the night?"

But it wasn't.

"Do you want it prepared?"

It. So he was making the call from the dungeon itself.

"Put it on show," Aled said, wondering if he was on speakerphone. "I'll want to inspect it first. I'll be round in about forty minutes."

"Pleasure doing business with you."

Aled snorted as he hung up, then sat up and thumbed out a text.

Me: How is he?

He didn't expect an immediate reply. They were clearly still mid-scene. So he tossed the phone aside and went to find his shoes. He'd showered and changed after work but was going for the casual look. The kind of guy who used a sex slave to wank into, rather than one who had a particularly sadistic streak.

It just felt...odd, to be physically cruel when Gabriel had been so twitchy about reforming their rules. In a way, Gabriel's desperation for a hard game would help. Aled didn't have to mete out the violence when he was still uncomfortable, but whatever he *did* do would still hurt in the aftermath of a savage beating from Kevin. Gabriel would get the violence he craved and Aled could ease back into it.

Win-win.

The phone lit up again just as he locked the front door, but Aled waited until he'd cleared the new snow off the car before sinking into the driver's seat, turning on the heaters and swiping open the new message.

Kevin: He's fine. Heavy game but nothing broken and won't need any stitches. Spaced out twice so he's drifting, don't go overboard on the punishment if he's a bit slow. Might want to keep an eye on his back if you fuck him.

Me: Got it, thanks.

Spaced was good. Drifting was good. Gabriel didn't let himself space very often and it was like a drug all on its own. He was phenomenally beautiful when he just let go like that and Aled lived for those scenes.

And if he'd done it twice under Kevin's hand, he was bound to do it again for Aled.

Aled drove leisurely. The weather was foul, the snow turning to icy sleet, so it was almost ten by the time he reversed up Kevin's driveway. Kevin opened the back door just as he killed the engine, and took Aled to the basement through a quiet and sleeping house.

"Everything all right?" Aled asked as he unlocked the top door.

"Yeah, he was fine," Kevin said. "Just a bit pent-up, I reckon. You know what he's like."

Aled cracked a smile. "Any damage?"

"Whipped him until he safeworded, so his back is a mess. I've already cleaned and checked the cuts, though. He shouldn't need anything."

Aled nodded then schooled his expression and strengthened his stance as Kevin unlocked the bottom door and showed him into the basement.

It was a sex dungeon. No two ways about it. Aled had only been down here once or twice before and it changed reasonably regularly. A new St Andrew's cross had been installed on one wall and the tin tub had been sunk into the floor. It bore the remains of a bloody ice bath and Aled gave an involuntary shiver.

There was a dining room chair laid on the floor, its back resting on the cold stone. Gabriel's arse was propped on the lip of the seat, his thighs secured to the front legs with zip ties so that his arse and cunt were on full display. He'd been waxed before use and Aled patted the smooth skin curiously. There was no sound — and Gabriel could make them. He was blindfolded but not gagged. His arms were tied in the small of his back and the side of his head lay on the ground. He wasn't tied to the back of the chair, but then, Aled supposed he wouldn't have the strength to right himself or the frame he'd been lashed to.

And Kevin hadn't been kidding about the mess.

"Interesting set-up. Could I fuck it like that?"

"Only when you're ready to throw it away. Probably break its back if you tried."

Aled hummed, patting the upraised arse again.

"Good for teaching it a lesson, though. It sucks dick good and proper after an hour like that."

Kevin stooped and seized a fistful of Gabriel's hair. He hauled him—and the chair—upright like that, and Aled saw blood bubble over the edge of teeth as Gabriel fought not to cry.

"It's quiet."

"It learns."

Aled grunted. "Come on, then. Where's the sales patter? I'm not paying your prices for any old thing."

"Because I sell quality. Look at it." Kevin wrenched Gabriel's head back and rubbed a thumb around his bleeding lips. "Got a mouth like a Dyson. Looks good hanging off cock, whichever end you stick it."

"It's damaged," Aled said.

Gabriel didn't so much as twitch at the harsh pronoun and Aled smirked to himself. He'd tried 'it' once and only once and had nearly had his head ripped off. He'd have to remember this.

"It'll heal. First-time slave. It had ideas above its station. It's a screamer, too—I have a good selection of gags and chokers if you're interested."

"Oh, I have all I need on that front. May I?"

"Go ahead. No free fucks, though. Got others interested online. If you don't want it, I can find another buyer."

"I'm not interested in pretty," Aled said, circling Gabriel. "I need functional. Pretty things break, in my experience. I'm not buying at your prices for something that'll break in a few weeks."

"It's been fully tested. It's not going to break."

Aled put the chair back down, although not as quickly or roughly as Kevin had righted it. He'd never tied Gabriel to a chair quite like that before and he examined the way Kevin had done it before he examined Gabriel himself. He'd been washed. Used — thoroughly, by the loose grip and lack of whimper at the rough intrusion of dry fingers — but then scrubbed clean. Aled massaged, watching Gabriel's mouth working soundlessly, before withdrawing and using Gabriel's mouth to clean his fingers.

"It's breakable," he said. "You can't go selling it as pretty when you've ripped apart its back like that. And it's looser than a Holbeck whore. I'll not pay more than half for it."

"Half? It gets wet the minute you wave a cock at it. It's worth double what I charge in the first place!"

"Doesn't need to be wet to fuck it."

"Test it out, then. Fuck its face, see how pretty it looks on your cock."

"Like I said, I'm not interested in pretty. Half or nothing."

"I'll knock ten percent off, for the marks."

"It's bleeding!"

"Twenty percent off, then."

They haggled, Aled carding his fingers through Gabriel's hair and watching his thighs shivering. Aled knew those signs. He was wet and itching to touch himself, but not permitted.

Aled finally took pity and agreed at twenty-five percent off their never-known, never-paid price. Gabriel was packaged up with duct tape, mouth and eyes bound to keep him blind and dumb, and dumped on the back seat of Aled's car under a blanket like a large parcel. Kevin silently handed over a plastic bag with his clothes then loudly offered one last piece of advice well within Gabriel's earshot.

"It likes to touch itself. I'd recommend a chastity belt when you're out, so it's not tempted."

That finally elicited a whimper from the back seat, and Aled smirked.

"What makes you think my toys get to keep their fingers?"

Kevin grinned.

Aled drove fast, deliberately jostling the back seat and braking too hard. He took the long route home and swung up into the garage nose-first rather than the usual reverse, just for the extra bounce and speed.

Then he left Gabriel to wait in the car while he unlocked the house and fetched a knife.

After all, removing duct tape from a new toy with scissors wouldn't be as fun.

He dragged Gabriel out of the car and onto the garage floor and let him feel the blade when cutting him out of the bonds. He left the blindfold and gag in place for the moment, leaving Gabriel exposed and vulnerable as he was steered, blind and naked, into the house and up the stairs into the master bedroom.

Gabriel would be expecting to be shoved to his knees and face-fucked — so for that reason alone, Aled didn't give it to him. Instead he lifted Gabriel up onto the bed, arranging him on his back with his arms folded up against his chest to secure and hide his breasts. Kevin had finally put Aled in the mood for something a little rougher, though, so rather than ribbon, he went for the wire. It was thin metal twine, gold, the sort used to hang pictures. Rough when rubbed against the skin, and an encouragement to keep as still as possible.

Which meant, when being fucked against it, bearing down as hard as possible and meeting every thrust with tight resistance.

Gabriel whined against the gag as Aled wound the gold tighter and tighter, digging it into the soft skin of his armpits and elbows, twisting it in patterns along his belly and back, looping it around his neck like a makeshift collar, ensuring that his nipples were surrounded in the cruel twists. With every cry, Aled slapped him, swatting over the wire to press it in harder, until the lesson was learned and quiet swept in again, broken only by Gabriel's harsh breathing and the gentle creaks of the mattress as Aled worked.

And when Gabriel was completely bound from waist to neck in wire, Aled took him by the knees and dragged him down the sheets.

A yell.

A squirm.

Then another shuddering cry and sudden stillness.

"I'm not much one for my toys moving around," Aled said in a deceptively soft voice. "I like them to stay still while I use them."

He spread Gabriel's knees wider and planted his hands on both feet to hold them down.

"Very pretty," he said and watched Gabriel's muscles tighten in reply. "Do you understand what happened this evening? I'm your owner. Which means your body belongs to me now. Every single part of it. If you want to use it, then you ask my permission. When I want to use it, you obey. Understood?"

He received a shaky nod.

"Good. Stay still."

When he let go, Gabriel remained perfectly still. Aled smiled, admiring the picture, and took a quick snapshot with his phone. He texted it to Kevin before setting the device aside and stripping off his jeans and underwear. He left his shirt in place as protection from the wire.

Then, without warning, he ripped the duct tape from Gabriel's mouth.

Gabriel yelled. His lips were flushed red and swollen and Aled leaned down to catch his chin in one hand and kiss them. They yielded instantly, opening up beneath his own, and Aled plundered, stealing air and sense, before climbing back onto the bed and dragging Gabriel down again until the swell of his arse was sitting pretty in Aled's lap, open and ready for the taking.

But Aled had other plans first.

Gabriel was hard, his thighs shivering. His dick was swollen, flushed and red. Damp, when Aled touched his fingers to hot skin and began to rub.

Gabriel's cry was nothing short of desperate. He rutted, hips lifting in Aled's lap, desperate for friction. The wire twisted and tightened and the cry turned to a sob. But the shuddering didn't stop. He attempted to close his knees and grind. He begged in a stream of words for more. He cried, thrashing, then cried harder as the wire cut into his flesh. And Aled said nothing, merely held his knees down and touched him, rubbed him, jerked in short, sharp bursts with the pads of his fingers, massaged and squeezed and *twisted* —

"If you come before I am inside you," he said casually as Gabriel began to scream, "then I will strap you to the bed and fuck your arse completely dry."

The scream turned into a frantic sobbing. Begging. Aled was elevated to sir, master, even lord. He was offered permanent servitude, given the right to imprison Gabriel in his bed and on his cock for the rest of his life, permitted to keep him in chastity belts and chains if only he would let Gabriel come, if only, if only —

"What are you?"

"*Yours!*"

Aled thrust home. He buried his dick in tight, hot heat. He clamped his mouth over bloody, abused lips. And with his other hand, holding Gabriel's pleasure between finger and thumb —

He pinched down.

Gabriel came. That caught body shuddered and jerked, pinned on Aled's cock and trussed in harsh wire. His heartbeat was bouncing out of his neck. His legs were clamps around Aled's hips. He clung and was held down, and Aled fucked through the pressure, fucked the shivering mess of pleasure and pain beneath him, fucked into a grip so tight it hurt amid the helpless body of a man he had ripped apart, stripped down to nothing but flesh and pleasure, and —

He barely pulled out in time. He came on Gabriel's hips and thighs, arms shaking as he held himself up. He breathed, open-mouthed, over Gabriel's tied belly, then sat back and stared at the mess before him, bound and helpless in wire and blood and cum. Legs open. Ready for more.

Aled laughed breathlessly and began to smooth his seed into sweat-soaked skin.

"Not bad, for such a new toy," he murmured, and brushed his lips over Gabriel's knee. "Now, let's see what else you've learned."

* * * *

Aled's chest felt tight.

He'd noticed that when ending the game and cleaning up, but it felt even tighter down in the kitchen. His fingers were shaking slightly on the knife as he chopped the parsley. He couldn't quite catch his breath.

His first wild thought was that the bacon butties had caught up to him and he was having a heart attack, but then he braced his arms against the counter and dropped his head to breathe. No, this was no heart attack. Panic, perhaps, but not heart.

The way Gabriel had whimpered when Aled had —

God.

He swallowed spasmodically and had to put a hand over his mouth. Fuck. Oh, *fuck.* He'd just let a man beat his partner into a bloody mess, then taken him home and fucked him again. There was blood all over the bed from Gabriel's back. And Aled had turned him over and rubbed his face in it, and —

"Aled?"

He closed his eyes at the soft voice. Then there were warm fingers on his arm.

"What's wrong?"

Aled took a shaky breath. It was bullshit. It *was.* Gabriel had — he'd liked it, he *had* —

"*Aled.*"

He looked. Gabriel had showered, his hair wet and spiky. He had dark red marks on his throat where the wire had throttled him. He was drowning in Aled's dressing gown, bare feet white splashes on the tiles, and he looked so bloody *vulnerable* —

"Think maybe I need a bit of aftercare," Aled croaked hoarsely and the fingers tightened slightly on his elbow.

"Oh. *Oh*, okay. C'mere."

The hug was somehow both soft and hard at the same time. Gabriel's skin was hot and damp. He was small and thin under the heavy robe and yet his grip was tight and reassuring. He held on. He opened up and clung. He didn't shrink back, he didn't—

"Want to go to the chair?"

Aled tightened his grip. "In a minute."

"No, c'mon. Chair. Then you can have a full-body hug. Legs and all."

Aled cracked a faint smile but still shook his head. "Just—"

"*Now*, Aled."

The order scraped along the edges of the attack, cracking it, and Aled let go. He was towed by the wrist into the living room and found himself in the cuddle chair before he quite knew what had happened. Gabriel settled, legs slung over Aled's lap, weight hot and hard against Aled's ribs and arms, face pressed to Aled's ear to kiss it. An arm locked around his shoulder and chest, the hug firm and blanketing, and Aled—

Breathed.

He took a deep breath, feeling as if it was the first since the scene had ended, and released it in a long, exhausted sigh.

"Talk to me," Gabriel murmured.

Aled spread his hand over one bare thigh, sliding it down to tuck into the crook of Gabriel's bent knee. There was a faint pulse there, too, plodding away without a care in the world. Slow. Calm.

Aled tried to copy it.

"C'mon, biscuit. What's up?"

The rarely used, usually mocking endearment surprised a chuckle from Aled's chest. He sighed and turned his face into Gabriel's, getting a kiss on the end of the nose for his efforts. It crackled on the surface of his fears, like a sparkler in the dark.

"The usual," he admitted finally. "I just came down, and that voice in the back of my head started up. That what I just did was—was no different to what abusers do."

"Except for the bit where nobody wants abusers to do it. I wanted you to do that."

Aled swallowed. "I know. I do."

"You're just not feeling it very well right now, huh?"

Aled smiled faintly. They both knew that headspace. Logic and emotion had very little to do with one another, and nowhere highlighted that more than kinky sex games. He knew he'd not done anything Gabriel hadn't wanted. He knew it. But—

There was always a *but*, lurking in the back of his head, ready to attack at a moment's notice.

And this was one of those moments.

"Yeah."

A kiss was pressed to his temple and Aled buried his face in the warm expanse of Gabriel's neck. He smelled of soap and sex. His fingers were gentle in Aled's hair, stroking a pattern into the scalp.

"I never thought I'd like having sex in picture wire, you know."

That surprised a laugh from Aled.

"I know my safewords. And I'd have used them if I didn't want you to do something."

"I know," Aled murmured.

"Did you need them?"

"No. It's just—just when I was making dinner. I was all right until then."

"Mm, maybe we should have cuddled in bed longer."

"Yeah," Aled murmured.

The bed had been ruined, and Gabriel's back had gone from kinky hurt to actual hurt, so they'd only snuggled for a few minutes when the game was over. They usually stayed longer. They usually cuddled until they fell asleep, or one of them got too hungry to stay. And it was always for Aled. Gabriel very rarely needed it, but Aled always did. Maybe that had been it. Maybe that was why Aled felt so damn adrift.

"You going to be okay?"

"Yeah," Aled murmured. "I think I just tried to come down too quickly. I'm okay."

It was better, here. With Gabriel warm and heavy in his lap, cuddling into his shoulder as though he owned Aled's soul. Playing with his hair and idly tracing patterns on him. He'd start making stupid jokes soon, trying to lighten the mood. And it would work, and eventually Aled would unlock enough to be able to laugh.

Then it would be over. Just a stupid thought, like all the other stupid thoughts.

It didn't make them any less gut-wrenching in the split second when they felt like they weren't stupid at all.

"I love what we do," Gabriel murmured softly. "I love what you and Kevin do. I love that he can rip me apart and you can take me home and put me back together, and when it's over and we're exhausted and fucked-out, you'll spoon up against my back and we'll cuddle and make fun of a TV show. And in the morning, he'll have sent me a selfie with Gabby, and he'll ask how we're doing and call me a slob because I've left stains on his nice clean floor."

Aled chuckled weakly.

"That floor wasn't clean."

"It was when I got there."

"Dirty git."

Gabriel kissed his cheek and Aled smiled, finally opening his eyes to stare at the ceiling. The ragged edges were smoothing out. Tiredness was creeping in. He wanted to eat a horse, then sleep for a thousand years.

Instead, he squeezed.

"Thank you," he murmured. "I needed that. And to be told off."

"Yeah, well, you need telling off sometimes. Your brain's a twat."

"Oi!"

"It is! Making shit up like that. Hey. How d'you feel?"

The question caught Aled by surprise, and he huffed a laugh, nudging his nose against Gabriel's.

"Safe," he said finally. "In control. Calmer."

"What'll it take to get all the way to calm?"

"You being a bossy bitch and making me wait on you hand and foot?"

"Done. Pick me up, Jeeves, and take me to the kitchen. Bitch needs feeding."

Aled laughed, working an arm under Gabriel's thighs and staggering up. The weight and angle were too much, but he forced his back the rest of the way and earned a kiss to the side of his head for the effort.

"How do I feel?"

The whisper was barely there.

Aled swallowed.

"You love me."

"Bingo."

The band around his chest dissolved, and Aled grinned. "What are you?"

Gabriel laughed, wriggling. Aled tightened his grip, and Gabriel stilled again with a small, breathy noise.

"Yours. Sir."

"Good."

"Always yours."

Chapter Sixteen

Gabriel woke up on Christmas morning to find that his first gift was Aled's erection digging into his hip.

Aled was still asleep but stirred when Gabriel started to jack him. His eyes were muzzy with fatigue, his expression soft and adoring when Gabriel kissed him, and suddenly a quick Christmas morning hand job felt disappointing.

The pleased noise Aled made when Gabriel straddled his lap sent a warm flush through Gabriel's chest that was nothing to do with sex. He sank down onto Aled's cock slowly but wasn't allowed to sit proudly atop his conquest for long—Aled soon sat up against the pillows, and drew him in to gnaw at his neck and murmur sleepy endearments that Gabriel would ordinarily have rebelled against. It was idle, affectionate and took a long time to reach its conclusion. And the climax was more of a gentle hill than a mountain, more of a fall than a high to be chased. It swept over Aled silently, the rush of heat inside Gabriel the only clue it was over, and his own followed when Aled touched him, gentle as a sigh when settling down to sleep.

If sex *did* have to be vanilla sometimes, Gabriel could accept a bit of sweetness to the flavour.

The kisses weren't nearly so sweet, though, and eventually he took himself off to the bathroom to brush his teeth.

After a long shower and trimming his beard back down to stubble, Gabriel set out in his towel and rediscovered Aled in the kitchen making breakfast. They swapped much nicer kisses against the counter, and Gabriel fended off the attempted towel stealing until after they'd eaten, at which point he was pressed up against the fridge and insistent hands vanished under the Egyptian cotton.

"You'll be — fuck — late," he said breathlessly as Aled sucked on his neck.

"Well, I pride myself on never coming early…"

"Tit — *oh*. I mean to visit your nan."

Aled chuckled in his ear. "That's tomorrow."

Gabriel blinked, the lusty haze dissipating. He pushed. Aled stepped back, looking confused.

"Everything okay? You usually like it when I pinch your — "

"You're not going to your nan's today?"

"No. Boxing Day. She's going to my uncle's for the day."

"Your uncle?"

"Er, yes? Her son? My dad's brother? Do you want a family tree?"

"I didn't even know you had an uncle," Gabriel said stupidly.

"We don't get on," Aled said.

"Define don't get — "

"In the same way you don't get on with your mum."
Oh.

Gabriel's grandfather and uncles lived in Pudsey, but it was a coincidence. He was from down south. And all the rest of his family—headed by his die-hard transphobe of a mother—had stayed there. Two hundred odd miles was still uncomfortably close, in Gabriel's opinion.

"We take turns," Aled said carefully. "I visited Nan last Christmas, so this time I'll go tomorrow and Paul will go today."

"Oh. I thought—I thought you'd spend the day with her, like last year. And I'd just go up to Grandpa's like usual."

"Well—" Aled lightly tweaked the towel opening. "If you want to go, I'll drive you up there. But I was hoping to spread you out on the bed and pull my cum back out of you with my fist."

Blood shot to Gabriel's groin.

"Um—"

"Up to you if we make it gentle." Aled's breath was hot on his ear and there was a single finger tracing Gabriel's lips. And not the lips on his face. "Or not."

"I already showered," Gabriel whispered. "It's gone."

"I see."

The finger breached him. Gabriel sucked it a breath as it teased him with the dangerous, hard sensation of an uncut fingernail.

"I'll just have to put some more there instead, won't I?"

* * * *

"I'll see you tomorrow," Gabriel promised as Aled padded back into the bedroom. "Yep. Merry Christmas, Grandpa. Bye."

He held up the phone and felt it plucked from his fingers. Didn't see, because Aled had blindfolded him the minute he'd started the call.

"Everything okay?"

Sure. Grandpa wasn't the sentimental type to really care if Gabriel visited or not, and he wasn't especially close to his uncles. They'd done him a favour years ago, and he repaid it by visiting sometimes and helping out with Grandpa. That was all. A relative-free Christmas was a nice prospect for all involved.

"Yep."

His lips were teased apart by Aled's in a damp kiss, and Gabriel lifted his head for more.

"Ah-ah. You just lie there. I'm going to watch my Christmas present and explore the other."

They had swapped presents — a jumper for Gabriel, the latest superhero film on DVD for Aled — then had sex on the living room floor. Then Aled had plugged him with a screwed-up ball of wrapping paper, and told him not to leak on his way upstairs.

And so here he was. Blinded and lying naked on the sheets, feet on the pillows and head at the bottom of the bed. Wedged painfully open with silver wrapping paper and drifting in a sea of cotton that dipped as Aled perched on the edge of the mattress.

"You want any restraints?"

Gabriel shook his head. He sensed Aled come closer, then a kiss was pressed to the inside of each wrist.

"If you want to get off while I'm doing this, go ahead."

"Okay."

"I'll suck you off if you want, too, but no prick."

"'Kay."

He earned himself another one of those coaxing, wet kisses, then one leg was lifted and the bed dipped as Aled settled between his ankles. The TV was switched on. The DVD menu beeped gently to itself and some dramatic music for presumably undramatic studio logos started up in the quiet bedroom.

"Seriously?"

"I'm going to take my time," Aled said.

Gabriel flexed his toes, then his cunt as the paper was worked free. He grumbled and Aled laughed gently.

"Want me to kiss it better?"

"Yes, please."

The first kiss on his labia was a chaste mockery of the ones to his wrists, but teeth and tongue soon began to tweak his lips and pussy. He was still in a post-orgasmic haze from the fuck on the rug downstairs and whined when Aled began to suck. It was over quickly.

Then, before his breathing had even settled, Aled began to finger him.

If Aled's cock was good and his mouth was sinful, his hands had once belonged to Satan. Getting fingerfucked by Aled could be anywhere between painful torture from a sadistic monster to a loving stroke that was barely felt but for the climax it teased out of him. Aled could be clinical or caressing, brutal or brilliant. He could make it as sexy as a visit to the gynaecologist or reduce Gabriel to nothing but a pulse and the word 'yes' on repeat.

Gabriel relaxed at the familiar touch. A single finger, gently working at his lips until they were wet, then drying itself in long strokes up and around his dick before smoothing its way back down. A shivery pleasure followed it, ghosting along his skin and sinking into his nerves. He sighed with every touch to his cock. Eventually, Aled settled his weight along Gabriel's right leg, kissing his belly briefly before turning his attention to the film, the pattern of pierce, stroke, tease, stroke, repeat settling into a rhythm between Gabriel's legs.

And Gabriel —

Drifted.

He felt as if he was a body of water, Aled dipping into him like a swimmer on the edge of a pool. But he also felt as though he was a balloon, ready to float away but for the weight anchoring his leg to the bed. He reached blindly for the footboard and opened his knees wider.

"More," he whispered.

"Patience," Aled chided, but he let Gabriel have a little more. The first gentle finger was joined by another and they stroked up either side of him to meet again at his cock with every pass. Nails dragged against the folds of his skin until he felt scored open, and they wriggled into him in tiny bursts of movement until they were buried to the final knuckle and he could feel them inside.

That was the best part.

It was oddly non-sexual. He could come on cock, but it wasn't the way the world ended. Coming from the inside was just vaguely pleasant but coming from the outside would shatter him into a thousand pieces, like an imploding star that went too far and burst again in every direction, spilling stardust into the universe for all eternity.

But the feeling of something simply being inside? The pressure against him? The heat nestled into his muscles? He squeezed and felt Aled wave his fingers in reply. He relaxed and they curled soothingly into him. He could feel the fingerprints left against the hard wall to the back, and the loving curiosity in the strokes that pushed into the front and sides and tested his limits, opened him up, kissed him from the inside.

Some war raged from the TV on the wall. A burst of gunfire and a snide remark made Aled chuckle. But Gabriel just closed his eyes behind the blindfold and centred himself on the hand that cupped him inside and outside, and held him like he was a new country to be discovered, a universe otherwise unknown, and the most beautiful thing that these intrepid explorers had ever seen.

It was sensual pleasure, to be gently worked open on loving hands with no other intention. Even when the drying cum was worked back out of him and his hiss of discomfort was met with a shift in weight and the wet seal of lips around his cock, Gabriel felt less sexual pleasure and more a strange, hedonistic bliss. He was cocooned in cotton, brought to the peak of the mountain by a lover's mouth and kissed back down to earth by the same lips that had dragged him away from it. Lips that tracked from cunt to chin. Soft. Loving. He opened to the kiss and tasted himself, and his only reply to the murmured question was to tighten his grip around the three fingers now searching out every nerve inside him and squeeze them back into one.

"Does that mean fine?"

"Mhmm…"

For the longest time, that was all that was there. Three fingers, sometimes clutched as one and sometimes fanned out to stretch him. They pushed in and dragged out, over and over again, until he made a grumble about dry discomfort and a bottle cap popped.

Then the fire came.

The label called it a warming tingle. Gabriel called it bottled sex. The heat lit him up like a firework, and he sobbed as his dick was pumped between finger and thumb until it hurt, everything hurt, *coming* hurt—

"Empty," he whispered into the dark. "Fuck, please, m'empty, please—"

"Ssh…"

His knee was pushed over to open him up wider. He'd come like a burst water main, and it was all pushed back inside. From very far away, he heard the noise, but couldn't scrounge up a scrape of embarrassment. He was being wrought open, dissolved like gold melting in the forge. He was nothing. Boneless, limp, a puddle of *nothing*.

Knuckles bumped against his shores, and he rocked as though caught in the tide.

"I love you."

Aled's voice was the wind that plucked white from the waves and his hand was the shore that Gabriel crashed down on. The air rushed out of his lungs as the emptiness was banished. As he was filled. As the thin wedge that had been driven into him began to turn and he felt—from the inside—every tiny bone twisting in Aled's wrist.

"Aled."

"Mm?"

"Hand."

He grasped blindly, and his fingers were taken in a familiar grip. His knuckles were kissed then his mouth. He gasped around the kiss as Aled tightened his biceps, and *power* surged down his arm and into Gabriel's body, as tangible as any load he'd ever taken.

"F'k me."

"What?"

"F'k me."

"Just relax, sweetheart."

He basked in Aled's voice. Turned his face into the kisses that came out of the dark and sighed as movement fluttered inside him, like mermaids swimming in the deep, as fingers fanned out and the wide span of rigid knuckles eased. Then they closed and the fist was clenched again. Sank a little deeper. Relaxed. Fanned out. Clenched —

It was like fucking, but without the sex. Gabriel wasn't moving and yet the whole bed was shaking. He was being rocked in the centre of the world, the tide caused not by the moon but by the fist sinking impossibly farther into him until it met the sharp edge of warning, where nothing — not even his limits — dared to cross.

Then it stilled.

Relaxed.

Curled up inside him like he was a pocket.

"Hey."

Gabriel hummed, blinking hazily under the cloth. It was dark. Why was it dark?

"You wanna come like this?"

"Mhmm…"

"Is that a yes?"

He didn't answer. He dragged his foot higher on the bedspread and felt everything change inside, yet stay the same. It had been agony before. Fistfucked until he bled. But this was —

"C'mere."

The kiss was soft and messy. Someone was dying on the TV. Gabriel could sympathise, but why were they complaining about it? If he was dying, then it was the best thing to have ever happened.

"You are so stoned right now…"

"Mmm…"

"Could stay like this until the credits roll, you know."

"F'k me through it…"

The hand tightened in its pocket and the gentlest of undulations rippled through him, like a stone thrown into a rock pool. It barely moved, and yet the ocean flowed from him. It barely moved, yet what remained dissolved.

He was everything and nothing, all and none, the world and an atom. This was love without sex, and sex without love, and all the points along either line.

But it was Aled.

Aled who held him, Aled inside him, Aled around him. Aled-Aled-Aled.

It occurred to him — as Aled's fingers flexed inside him, as Gabriel's entire being was wrapped around this man physically as well as mentally, as he was moved like the sea yet surrounded by another — that the two-week trial would over in a matter of days.

And Gabriel didn't want to leave.

Chapter Seventeen

Aled hated working between Christmas and New Year. It had been the perfect Christmas. The day itself had been spent with Gabriel, and the day after laughing at Nan's scathing assessment of her younger son, and the day after *that* catching up with Suze over a pint about their respective celebrations with their partner — him — and their future in-laws — her.

But then the wet, miserable week between the two holidays rolled around and Aled ended up having to go into work.

"At least *you* earn decent money. No minimum wage for you," was Gabriel's unhelpful reply, so Aled gave him half a blow job then left him hanging before heading to the office. By the time he'd pulled up outside the building, his phone was full of swearwords and aspersions on his parents' marriage.

Me: Love you too, darling x

The only upside of working that week was that there was very little to do. Most of their sister firms were closed over Christmas, so there was no marketing to actually be done. The Christmas campaigns had been up and running for weeks, and there was nobody to talk to about making new ones. He spent most of the morning cleaning out his email folder, playing games on his phone and helping one of the secretaries decorate the CEO's office for his birthday next week. He'd never been paid so much to draw stars on Post-it notes before, and it made a nice change.

But he missed Suze.

She wasn't going to be back until after New Year and even ringing her for a chat at lunch wasn't the same. Half the fun of watching Suze rant was *seeing* her. She waved her hands and pulled faces and had the most expressive eyes. Just hearing about her future mother-in-law wasn't the same.

Then the incoming call warning beeped.

"Hang on, Suze. Got another call incoming."

"It'll be the boss, tell him to go away!" she shouted as he took the phone away from his ear and frowned at the display.

What the –

"It's Gabriel," he told her. "I'll ring you back."

Gabriel very rarely rang him. And he'd be at home, so why bother?

"Hello?"

"Aled?"

Gabriel's voice was very quiet and hoarse, and Aled's stomach twisted. "Yeah, it's me. What's up, babe?" The endearment slipped free, and when Gabriel didn't huff about it, Aled's stomach clenched even harder.

"Work called." Gabriel sniffed and it sounded like he was trying to snort half a pound of cocaine. "I'm unemployed."

"Oh, hell."

"They're closing the store. They've sacked everyone. I've got no job anymore."

"Hey, it's all right," Aled interrupted, lowering his voice to a soothing murmur. He sat forward, dropping his feet to the floor from where they'd been propped on the desk. Cheryl, the secretary, gave him a worried look. "It's all right. When's your notice up?"

"Two weeks."

"Okay, that's two more weeks pay, and a fortnight to find something else. You can do that. And —"

"What if I can't, Aled, I'll lose the flat, and —"

His voice was rapid and panicked. Aled sympathised. It had been a long time since he'd had to worry about money, but he remembered the feeling. His parents hadn't been particularly well off. University had been a juggling act of begging, borrowing and trying not to resort to stealing. He could remember lying awake at night wondering how he was going to make ends meet, and what would happen if he couldn't.

"If you can't, I'll help you," Aled interrupted. "It's not the end of the world. I know it's fucking scary and it's shit they've done this to you, but you could always find something better, with less weird shift patterns, and more than the minimum wage. Could be a blessing."

Gabriel swallowed, and Aled realised uneasily that he was crying.

"Hey, you at home?"

"In town."

"Wakefield?"

"Yeah."

"Let me come and pick you up."

"You're working—"

"I'll tell them I'm sick."

"No." Gabriel's voice was croaky, but firm. "You can't put your job on the line for me."

Aled bit his lip. "It wouldn't," he said gently. "They'll be fine without me for half a day. There's nothing going on anyway. Let me come and pick you up."

"You don't need to—"

"I want to. You're upset, and I'm worried about you, okay? You never call me—you're a text demon."

It didn't elicit a laugh like usual and Aled grimaced.

"Where are you?"

"Trinity Walk."

"Okay, why don't you go to the Costa behind Sainsbury's and get yourself a coffee or something sweet. I'll come and get you, then I'll take you home and make a big fuss of you, all right?"

Gabriel swallowed again. "Full body massage?"

"From your toes to your scalp," Aled promised.

"Okay."

He hung up and Aled dropped his phone on the desk, stooping to unplug the charger.

"I have to—"

"I heard," Cheryl said. "Was that your girlfriend?"

"Yeah," he lied, not bothering to correct her. "Bad news. Look, if—"

"Oh, you're around, I've seen you," she said airily, waving a hand. "You know Aled, he's probably flirting with the girls down in finance again!"

Aled rolled his eyes but accepted the out, sweeping his things into his bag and grabbing his coat off the stand in the corner.

"You're a gem!" he shouted before the door banged shut behind him and he was taking the stairs two at a time down to the car park. Fuck. *Fuck.* They'd had such a great Christmas, and now this. *This.*

The city was heaving, and it took him a ridiculously long time to get back into Wakefield—which wasn't any better. The car park at Sainsbury's was packed out, and Aled cursed post-Christmas sales and the fact that Wakefield suddenly seemed to hold a population of six million whenever Primark was selling off their tat.

But there was one tiny reprieve from the mad crush.

Gabriel wasn't waiting in Costa, but at the bottom of the stairs up to Trinity Walk. He was nothing more than a shape smoking in the shadow of the concrete and Aled's heart twisted before he wrenched the car around and headed for the disabled bays opposite his dejected-looking partner.

"Hey," he called out the open window. "Room for one more in here."

Gabriel didn't so much as blink. Aled sighed, mentally apologised to whoever was watching and sloppily parked in a free yellow bay. Sliding out, he paced through the drizzle to the shelter of the stairs and watched the cigarette glow.

"How many?" he asked gently.

Gabriel dragged heavily on the stub he held between finger and thumb. "Fifth."

"You know what, in light of your shitty day, I'll not argue about the rest of the packet," Aled said quietly, sliding an arm around his waist. Gabriel relaxed against his jacket with a sigh, but didn't look up and didn't stub out the cigarette. "Come on, sweetheart. Snuff it out and let's go home."

"I won't have one."

The whisper was so quiet that Aled almost missed it. "You won't have what?"

"A home."

"What? Gabe—"

"Jobseekers won't cover the flat, they'll make me move into a council and last time I was in a council flat someone scrawled 'tranny paedo' on my front door and set fire to my bins." Gabriel's voice was wavering, razor-thin and cracking along the edges. "I'll lose the flat, Aled, and then it'll be lying awake, listening to kids spraying slurs on my front door, and then—I can't—I can't go back to the streets again, I *can't*, I—"

"Hey, hey, hey, ssh," Aled murmured, taking the cigarette and tossing it away. Gabriel turned into him, clinging, and Aled rocked them lightly on the spot, combing his fingers through the hair at the back of Gabriel's neck and head. "What do you mean, back to the streets?"

"I—I told you. I left home at sixteen."

"Yeah, and I assumed you had somewhere to go."

"No."

Aled closed his eyes. *Oh, Christ.* "So you were a sixteen-year-old kid living on the streets?"

"Yeah."

"Fucking hell, Gabe…"

"I ran away. I couldn't take it at home anymore, so I ran away. I lived in a fucking *box*, Aled, I literally lived in a box, I slept in doorways and underpasses until I met Jim, I can't do it again, I *can't*—"

"Okay, listen to me. *Listen!*" Aled barked, prising Gabriel free and shaking him. "Look at me. *Look.*"

Gabriel looked. His face was flushed red and his eyes were streaming, but he looked and Aled squeezed his shoulders gently.

"I'm not going to let someone that I care about end up in a box on the street. It's not happening, and that is *that*. Okay? So you don't have to be chain-smoking a whole packet of fags and crying out here, because all this is, is goodbye to a job you didn't really like, and time to find one that's less shit."

"But I can't afford —"

"I can," Aled said firmly. "Now how we do it is up to you, but you can either say fuck the trial period and stay with me until the job situation is sorted, or I can cover the shortfall on the flat until you have a new job. And if you do stay, I am not going to get pissed at you if once you've sorted another job, you want to move out again. This can be a permanent thing or it can be just until you've rearranged everything. I don't care. But you're not going back to some box, and I will not let you. All right?"

Gabriel's chest hitched before his face — cold and wet — was buried in Aled's neck and he was clinging viciously. Aled's chest ached. He knew very little of Gabriel's family. They had been dismissed in one conversation months ago as 'shit'. He knew that his mother was a transphobe and had thrown him out, and he knew that the relationship with his grandfather was only recently repaired. He knew that Gabriel had lived in Sheffield before Leeds and somewhere further south before that. But he hadn't known about the homelessness.

Shit, no wonder he was so antsy about the job. How could any family let a sixteen-year-old kid end up in a box? How could Gabriel think even for a second that would happen again now he had Aled in the picture? For fuck's sake, Aled's car was worth twenty thousand, thirty when he'd bought it. He could support a bloody cycling boyfriend for a *year* without too much trouble. How could Gabriel seriously believe he'd end up back in doorways and underpasses with Aled around? And even without Aled, what about Kevin? There wasn't a cat in hell's chance Kevin would allow it.

Aled took a deep breath.

Panic. That was what it was. It was panic. He was scared and panicking and he wasn't thinking rationally. Now wasn't the time to get pissed off and ask those questions. Now was the time for the promised fuss. Just like a scene gone wrong. Just like when a game missed the right note, and he had to find the right one again.

"Come on," he murmured, kissing the side of Gabriel's head. "Let me take you home, make a big fuss of you like I promised and wind you down."

Gabriel nodded, and silently allowed Aled to steer him through the rain to the car. He remained silent all the way out of the car park and onto the ring road, before croaking, "You can't."

"I can't what? Make a big fuss of you?"

Aled earned himself a wan smile, but Gabriel wasn't to be deterred. "You can't just pay all my rent and bills."

"I can stop my partner from losing his home and being forced back onto the streets."

"I'm not a pet to be kept."

Aled sighed. "No, you're not, and that's not what I'm doing."

"You're offering to pay for everything."

"And if you were my pet, or I were paying to keep you, then I would expect something in return. And we'd outline a new deal for that. But we're not. All I will be doing, no matter which option you pick, is providing a security net against losing your home."

"I'd be living in a flat entirely paid for by one of my regulars," Gabriel croaked and Aled winced, flicking on the indicator. "What — Aled, why are we going to Halfords?"

"We're not, I'm using their car park because buses get pissy round here if you use their stops," Aled quipped, and hauled on the handbrake. "Right," he said, twisting to face Gabriel. "Listen to me. I am not paying to keep you. I am not some fucking sugar daddy, or a pimp, or whatever other idea you've got in your head right now. All I am doing — *all* I am doing — is preventing someone I *love* from losing everything. I *can* afford to stop this, so I *will* stop this, you understand me?"

Gabriel simply stared at him, eyes wide and face pale.

"You're panicking. That's all. Deep down, you know I wouldn't let it happen. You know Kevin wouldn't let it happen either. You aren't going to fall. I *promise*, all right? And if you rang Kevin, he would tell you the exact same thing. I would do the exact same for Suze, I would even do it for Tom, and I will certainly do it for you."

Gabriel took a shaky breath. His fingers were shivering in his lap and Aled wanted to hold them.

"I'll be fucking dependent on you," Gabriel whispered. His face was painfully open, so anxious and afraid that it made Aled's heart hurt. "Don't — God, Aled, *please* don't make me regret that."

"Hey," Aled whispered, giving in and squeezing those shaking fingers. "I won't. All right? When you get a new job, the deal can be off or we can leave it in place and that decision will be one hundred percent yours."

Gabriel squeezed back and swallowed. "I — you can't pay for my flat, Aled. You can't. I'd just feel like a total whore, like I was some — some fucking prostitute, and you were paying for me to fucking entertain clients or something."

Aled grimaced.

"But the house, I don't know…"

"If you won't let me pay for the flat, then you are welcome at home," Aled said softly. "You could take the spare room if that would make you feel better or you could stay in with me and get squashed to death every morning when I get up."

"You take half an hour to get up," Gabriel croaked and Aled laughed.

"Be an hour if you're there *all* the time. These two weeks have been nothing."

"Oh, God."

"So is that it?" Aled prompted softly. "Give up the flat and move in until you've sorted everything out?"

Gabriel swallowed and nodded. Aled smiled, leaned over to kiss his cheek and put the car back into gear.

"All right," he said. "Enough planning. We can sort everything out tomorrow. Tonight, I'm going to take you home, make one of those cannelloni things you like so much and give you a scalp-to-toenail massage just like I promised at lunchtime. Okay?"

"Okay."

But Gabriel stared out of the window, silent and unmoving, the whole way home.

Chapter Eighteen

When Gabriel finally gave in to his need to piss, the sun was high in the sky outside Aled's bedroom window and the road was quiet.

But he could smell bacon.

Yawning, he crawled out of the bed and stumbled into the bathroom. He felt tired down to his very bones — and yet he also felt calm. A hell of a lot calmer than his embarrassing panic attack yesterday. Christ, what an *idiot*.

It was embarrassing. He'd just dissolved and started spouting all sorts of nonsense, and he rubbed a hand over his face, groaning, as he sifted through his memory. God, he'd all but accused Aled of being out to get him. It was a miracle Aled hadn't lost his temper, and Gabriel wouldn't blame him if he had.

Anyway, even if Aled was willing to let Gabriel go back on the streets, Kevin wouldn't. He shook himself. It was all about finding ways to make this comfortable, that was all. There'd be no boxes. No streets. He'd have *somewhere*.

They just had to figure out where.

And how.

He decided to go and find the bacon first, though. Stealing Aled's dressing gown from the back of the bathroom door and tucking his nose into the sleeve for a minute to inhale the familiar, soothing smell, he abandoned the bathroom and inched carefully down the stairs.

"Morning, sweetheart."

"Guess I wasn't imagining the bacon, then," Gabriel said.

"Nope."

"You should be at work."

"I have an awful case of the stomach flu."

"So you're making a full English?" Gabriel asked doubtfully.

"*They* don't know I'm making a full English." Aled grinned then lifted an arm. Gabriel shuffled under it for a hug, burrowing into Aled's side, and sighed contentedly when Aled kissed his hair. "You okay?"

"Mm."

"Any advance on that?"

Gabriel sighed. "Calmer. Less panicky about everything."

Aled squeezed. "Good. You were pretty wound up yesterday."

Understatement of the century.

"Everything just felt like it was getting on top of me — work, Michael, the flat…"

"And now?"

Gabriel stretched up to kiss Aled's cheek. "Got you. And somewhere to live. So — yeah, I've still got a roof over my head and food to eat. I can work on everything else."

"That's more like it. Speaking of eat, are you in the post-shot scary stage where I swear you have hollow legs, or the post-sleep yoghurt-is-a-healthy-breakfast stage?"

"Scary stage."

"Christ, grab another packet of bacon out of the fridge, then."

Three butties and a large coffee later, Gabriel felt a little more human and proposed going back to the flat to fetch the rest of his things. There was no point dragging it out. He'd have to ring the landlord. And they'd have to clear out more space for his clothes back here. Not to mention more bathroom space. Aled had left his whole linen cupboard behind, and Gabriel wasn't going the next few months without the good towels.

Pausing in the bedroom as he pulled the last of his clean T-shirts over his head, Gabriel eyed the open cupboard. Gabriel's jeans and muscle tees looked odd amongst Aled's jumpers, and he had the distinct feeling their socks were going to have polygamous orgies in the night and they'd never find a matching pair again, but it didn't feel so scary as when they'd started the trial. It didn't feel so overwhelming as it had when the text message had arrived from the boss.

He took a deep breath as he closed the wardrobe door and shook himself. This was *Aled*. Dangerous, domineering, completely sweet and goofy Aled. It was going to be fine.

"I was thinking," Aled called from the bathroom.

"Dangerous!" Gabriel shouted, dispelling his nerves by being obnoxious.

"Tit. I was thinking we could go and have a pub lunch after we've packed up your flat."

"You have stomach flu."

"We'll drive down to the Derbyshire. I doubt my boss has spies out in Bakewell."

"Can't we go to that pub in the Peaks? The one with the fireplace?"

"They've all got fireplaces out there."

Gabriel grasped for humour. Obnoxiousness and crass humour — it always worked before, and it would work again now to quell the butterflies in his stomach.

"The one where I blew you in the toilets that one time."

It worked. He smirked. Aled cackled with laughter.

"That doesn't narrow it down either, you slag."

Gabriel ducked into the bathroom to flip Aled off, who just laughed at him and washed away the remnants of his shaving foam.

"I know the one you mean. And you never know. Maybe I'll return the favour."

* * * *

Gabriel hadn't been back to the flat since they'd started the trial, and he had to wrestle with the lock before the door would open. Bills were piled up behind the door, some of them already red, and there was a vaguely damp smell.

And it looked — lonely.

Dust hadn't settled in the gaps where his bike usually stood, or the space for his missing alarm clock on the bedside table. The gentle dripping of the kitchen tap sounded deafeningly loud in the empty space. The closed curtains made it seem as if someone had died rather than just moved out.

Anxiety began to crowd back into Gabriel's head.

"I'll—I'll ring the landlord," he said awkwardly, fidgeting with his keys in the doorway. "Can you…"

He trailed off. Aled touched his elbow lightly.

"You okay?"

"Yeah."

Sort of. Maybe. It ached a little inside, having to ring Jack and explain the situation. The guy was an arse and Gabriel wouldn't miss him, but the rent had been cheaper than normal for Leeds. And it had been *his*.

That was the crux of it. He'd needed the low-income top-up every month to get by, and he'd sometimes let Kevin pay him to play a part in his porn movies when the bike needed some repair work or the weather was especially savage and he needed to put the heating on. He'd have been better off in a council flat.

But the flat had been *his*.

He hadn't liked the too-small bedroom. He'd hated the constant damp smell in the bathroom. The kitchenette was ugly, and the walls were paper-thin. In the winter, the windows frosted up from the inside. In the summer, he was cooked alive.

But it had been *his* tiny bedroom and damp bathroom. *His* ugly décor. *His* thin walls. He'd never really liked the place, but there was still a tearing feeling in his chest as he made his excuses to Jack.

"What was the rent?" Aled asked when Gabriel hung up and let out a shaky breath.

"Four hundred."

"My mortgage is three seventy," Aled said. "Once you've found work again, you can pay half."

"What's half of three seventy?"

"One eighty-five."

Gabriel swallowed. "Two hundred."

"What?"

"Two hundred. To — to help with the other bills too."

"Okay."

Gabriel rolled his head, deliberately working the tension out of his neck. It helped, a little. He wasn't thick — he knew full well why Aled had backtracked and asked for a rent payment. But it helped. He'd be paying *some* of his way. The sour feeling of failure eased a little in his gut.

A little. He'd always been a failure.

That was the biggest joke of the whole fiasco he'd made out of his life. No matter what he did, his mother's voice would always echo from the back of his mind and call him a failure. He'd not been enough to keep his father hanging around. He'd never been smart enough to go to college like his oldest sister, whose job kept them all in food and clothing when their respective fathers couldn't be bothered. And he'd failed at being a girl entirely. Failing was all he'd ever done. Part of him — the part that had his mother's nose — thought losing his job was just the universe reminding him of his place.

Then he slid down onto the bed beside Aled and sagged into his side for a hug. The warm touch banished the shrill chirping in his skull. Failure didn't find men like Aled. He'd be okay.

"Thank you."

"What's up?" Aled asked gently.

Gabriel sighed and opened the bottom drawer to start packing up his toy collection.

"This was the first flat that was mine," he admitted. "I told you that I ran away. Well, initially I was begging and squatting in London. Then I scrounged enough for a train ticket and I just picked the first train that was leaving. I got off in Sheffield and was begging in the bus station for a while until this PCSO got me into a hostel. He was nice," he added wistfully.

"Not gay?"

"Nope."

"Tragic."

"Yeah," Gabriel agreed with a faint smile. His name had been Jamie. He could remember his face and everything. One day, he'd have to track him down and thank him. "The hostel workers got me back into the social system and I got a job and a council flat and a phone. Started my whole Grindr thing. Then — then the neighbours at the flats figured out I was tranny scum, and put my door through and were calling me a paedo —"

Aled's arm locked around his waist. Warm. Tight. Secure.

"So the council shifted me, but it happened again. Even if I passed as a man for a while, they'd figure I was gay and do it anyway. Things calmed down a bit when my boyfriend moved in. I guess nobody wanted to tangle with him too much."

"Jim?"

"Yeah."

"Big lad?"

"Not really. Just a loudmouth. I don't know, he just had this air that he could hold his own in a fight. It was...peaceful, being with Jim."

"What happened there?"

Gabriel shrugged. "Nothing, really, we just didn't work out. I was like nineteen and I desperately needed the hormone therapy and top surgery. He got himself in massive debt paying for the HRT privately because the doctors wouldn't let me have it — said my lifestyle was too unstable — then we fell apart and I ran away to Leeds. I couldn't — Sheffield just — it was bad."

Aled tugged. Gabriel sagged into his side, sighing deeply.

"Take it he didn't pay for your boobs?"

Gabriel chuckled dryly. "He would have done. But I didn't want to lose those."

"He sounds nice."

"He was. He just — wasn't the one for me. It was all too monogamous and too serious. It sounds horrible, but I didn't love him. I liked him. He was fun. I liked being with him. But — I didn't *love* him, and he needed someone to love him."

"That's not your fault," Aled chided.

"Yeah," Gabriel murmured. "I just wish I had been older and not so dumb about it."

"So what happened then?"

"I came to Leeds. I lived with my uncles for a bit, but I hated it. And I refused to go back into council housing and Judith didn't want one of Kevin's other subs living with them long-term. I was stuck."

"Until you got your current job?"

"Yeah. I made a deal with Kevin that if things were really bad, he'd pay me for some of my video work with him to make up the shortfall."

He felt Aled's smirk against his scalp.

"I didn't realise Kevin actually made money off that."

"Oh, yeah. Loads. Live streaming and amateur movies and stuff. That's why Judith doesn't work — she usually does it, not me."

"Doesn't that trigger your whole hatred of being paid for sex?"

"It's Kevin. It's different."

Aled shrugged. Gabriel rolled his eyes and pulled away. He knew Aled didn't get that—truth be told, *Gabriel* wasn't sure he got it either—but the easiest thing about being with Aled was his casual acceptance. The man wasn't innately curious. He tended to just let things lie.

"This is the first place that was *mine*."

"I've never had a place that was just mine," Aled admitted. "I met my wife when we were still at school. I lived in student accommodation when I did my degree, then we bought the house together. I bought out her share when we divorced, so I suppose it's the first one that's mine too."

"Be—be ours again. If I stay."

"Yep."

"And if I don't?"

Aled shrugged. "I want you to, but if you don't, you don't."

Gabriel tipped back onto the bed. Aled let him go, and Gabriel stared up at him with a frown.

"Why are you so *easy*?"

"Because you're not," Aled replied, tapping his knee and shaking it lightly. "I figure the best way of keeping hold of you is not to hold on at all. You'll come to me when you're good and ready."

"You make me sound like a feral cat."

"You *are* a feral cat." Aled laughed and finally stood up. "Come on. Let's get everything packed and sorted."

The odd tension eased as they packed the rest of Gabriel's things—what little remained, anyway—into Aled's car, and Aled insisted on cleaning. Apparently it was some mortal middle-class sin to leave a rental place messy, and Gabriel barely managed to stop him going next door to borrow a vacuum cleaner for the carpet. And, quite frankly, the sight of his sometimes sadistic dominant flitting about with a *hanky* to clear dust off the windowsills gave Gabriel a stitch from laughing so hard.

"Watch it," Aled said as they locked up, Gabriel still giggling helplessly. "We can tank the lunch idea and I can beat you into a coma instead."

"Oh, please. You're too soft for a proper beating."

"I can send you back to Kevin. Retraining and all that."

Gabriel smiled, but there was no exciting thrill. He stretched up and kissed Aled briefly, and who cared if anyone saw? He'd not be back.

"Think I'd prefer something gentler today."

"Mm?"

"Yeah."

"After lunch," Aled said, patting Gabriel's bum affectionately. "Maybe we'll play with the ribbons again."

Gabriel hesitated at the communal door, looking back up the stairs one last time. Part of him wanted to stay. Part of him was scared. He'd settled down — for the first time, really, since he'd run away — but then Aled stroked his fingers, not quite taking his hand, and the anxiety eased.

Maybe it would be the start of something better.

"Don't look now," Aled murmured, "but Michael's car is hanging about."

Gabriel clenched his jaw. His wrist suddenly throbbed where Michael had grabbed it outside work. Without taking his eyes off the stairwell, he let the door swing shut and said, "After we put these bags in the boot, kiss me like it's a slushy movie."

"Make a show of it?"

"Yeah."

Aled chuckled. "Okay."

Gabriel didn't look, but he could see it out of the corner of his eye as they made for Aled's boot. The lights were on. The engine running. The hairs on the back of his neck prickled as he squashed the last of his things into the mess. He could *feel* Michael staring at him, and not in the sexy way that someone stared when they thought he was attractive. In the scary way. Like when chavs on the street figured out he was —

He shut the boot with a *thunk*, then turned and parked his arse against the number plate.

"This is the one and only time you get to do that," Aled said.

"What?"

"Put your bum on my car."

"Petrolhead."

"Guilty."

Gabriel beamed, obnoxiously wide like he was shooting a toothpaste ad, and looped his arms around Aled's neck, rocking up into him when familiar hands cupped his backside. One slid into his back pocket, and he arched. Aled really was only an inch or so taller than him, not enough for a proper craned-neck kiss, but Gabriel gave it his best shot.

He could *feel* the anger emanating from the other car.

And he could feel Aled's wry amusement in the way the kiss twisted around their smiles.

"You're a sod," Aled whispered, nudging their noses together. Gabriel, eyes closed, grinned.

"He deserves it."

"Yeah? Has he been calling you again?"

"No. Kevin came round looking for me, and Michael gave him some shit. So Kevin thumped him."

It was a very condensed version, but Gabriel knew he was asking for trouble right now if he told Aled about the scene outside the shop. His ploy worked. Aled chuckled and kissed his neck, burrowing his face against him for a moment before slapping his arse and pushing away.

"Come on, tart. Lunch."

"Fireplace pub and a blowjob?"

"I have a feeling that he's going to try following us, so fancy that place on the North Yorkshire moors we went last summer?"

Gabriel laughed as he opened the passenger door. "That's over an hour away!"

"Exactly."

Aled was right. Another engine roared alongside theirs, and they were tracked aggressively back to the motorway. Then Aled hit the northbound carriageway and put his foot down. And a ten-year-old Clio was no match for last year's Range Rover. Michael vanished from the rear view in a matter of seconds and took the ugly feelings with him.

"Okay?" Aled asked, and Gabriel stretched out in the passenger seat.

"Yeah. Yeah, I think so."

Chapter Nineteen

Aled didn't really do holidays.

His best Christmas in years had involved one present, a film, and fucking Gabriel with his fist for most of the day. He spent most New Year's Eves studiously avoiding work parties and playing loud music to drown out fireworks. And every year he tried — and failed — to get out of birthday drinks with Tom and Suze.

Failed being the operative word.

He knew he'd failed when he got home from work on his thirty-fifth birthday to find a note from Gabriel on the fridge, simply saying he'd gone to visit his granddad and would see Aled's hungover arse in the morning.

"Shit."

He'd been in Manchester all day for work at a product launch and hadn't bothered to check his phone before starting the drive home. Why would he? He'd either get home to food and sex, or Gabriel would be out and

Aled would make some food anyway and maybe have a wank on the sofa.

But no. Gabriel had taken his alcohol addiction out of the picture.

Which meant Tom and Suze were imminent.

Aled sighed and resigned himself to his fate, heading upstairs for a shower and a change of clothes. He heard the doorbell ring halfway through said shower and, by the time he stepped out, Suze had let herself in with her spare key and was singing in the kitchen.

"Five minutes!" he bellowed.

"You have two!" she shouted back.

He'd not seen her since Christmas, so he threw on some decent jeans and a T-shirt and headed downstairs sooner rather than later, catching her in a bear hug at the bottom of the stairs. Just like that, the little ache in his chest was soothed.

"Missed you," he told a mouthful of her peroxide blonde hair, and she tightened her grip.

"You too."

Tom was a friend. But Suze was *family*. And Cornwall was only five or six hours away, but Aled had missed her fiercely for the whole time she'd been gone.

Then she yelled, "Thirty-five!" and ruined his right ear.

"Thanks," he said sourly, letting go.

"And is this a permanent thing because that bike in your conservatory is definitely not yours," she said, wiggling her eyebrows and grinning up at him.

"Ah. Don't say anything."

The smile dimmed. "What?"

"Gabriel's lost his job," Aled said. "He didn't want to go back to council housing after some pretty grim experiences with them, so he's moved in here until it's sorted."

"Just until then?" she asked uncertainly.

"I hope for longer, but we've agreed up until then," Aled said. "Just don't say anything. He was a bit shaky about it."

She squeezed his arm. "But is it going okay?"

"Yeah."

"Oh, I know that face!"

Aled rolled his eyes and moaned at her, denying that he was loved up and shagged out. Even if his birthday *had* begun with fucking Gabriel over the kitchen counter without a rubber. He didn't have to tell *her* that.

He was dragged out for the usual crawl. Tom joined them at the second pub and got a round in. They called him old and domesticated, Aled pointed out that they were the same age and much more domesticated than he was, and everybody got drunk. *Very* drunk. By the time Gabriel texted him, the letters were blurry on a fuzzy screen and Aled struggled to unlock the phone to read the whole thing.

Gabriel: Can you call me?

Me: In the pub.

Gabriel: Please? Just step out for a couple of minutes. Won't take long.

Aled frowned and staggered to his feet, swatting away Suze's hands.

"Gotta ring Gabe."

"Why?"

"Dunno."

The cold air hit him full in the face as he stumbled outside and he blinked against the sudden flash of sobriety. A niggle of worry. Gabriel rarely called and even more rarely asked Aled to do it. The pub was quiet, Christmas celebrations having bitten several wallets too hard, and he leaned up against the wall just shy of the windows to put the phone to his ear.

And heard the ringtone.

"What the f —"

The sound was coming from the narrow alley that wound between the pub and the legal offices next door. As he stepped into the gloom, a hand snaked out and fisted in his collar. Gabriel's dark eyes glittered inches from his own.

"Hello," Aled said stupidly.

Gabriel said nothing. He simply towed Aled into the alley until they were hidden in the damp dark, then rubbed his entire body down Aled's front as he sank to his knees. Cold hit Aled's cock — then wet warmth.

"Oh Christ…"

He was worked. There was no other word for it. Gabriel sucked on him like their lives depended on it, and Aled was completely hard in under a minute. It was too dark to see, but he'd seen the sight plenty of times before. His memory could provide the lot. That dark head bobbing against him, flushed lips swelling around his prick, the flash of eyes as he looked up —

He cupped a hand behind Gabriel's head and pulled him closer. A throat caught against the head of his dick. Yielded. And the powerful drag of a submissive desperate to breathe was tugging on his cock with more power than a simple blow job could ever manage.

If the cold air had driven a few of the pints out of his system, the throat fuck did the rest.

Aled was practised at it. He choked Gabriel to the point of dizziness before letting go and three deep rasps were all that were allowed before he did it again. He didn't thrust. Didn't need to. A hand clenched in Gabriel's hair was more than enough and the fists clutching the knees of his jeans broadcast a silent permission across two years of alleyway fucks and questionable ethics.

Aled smiled at the dirty sky and closed his eyes.

Two years.

"Fuck," he whispered, and that was the only warning he gave.

The climax was nothing special. Satisfying, but not mind-blowing. But then Gabriel sucked him clean, nuzzling at his stomach before rising, and Aled caught him tight in a hug and bit his ear, careful not to kiss when there was still alcohol on his breath.

"Happy birthday," Gabriel whispered, nudging his jaw.

"I'm going to wake you up before I leave for work tomorrow and fuck you into a coma," Aled mumbled, squeezing tight before letting go. "Love you."

"You too, drinky. Go on. Go back to your pints."

"Oh shit, yeah, pints. I'll stay at Suze's. I'll—"

"Don't. I'm on my way to Kevin's," Gabriel said, nipping his ear. "Getting the train to Leeds then he's going to pick me up and we're going to a hotel."

"A hotel?"

"Yeah, he's got this friend."

Aled laughed. "I take it you've played with his friend before?"

"Well, duh. Anyway, the friend is playing with me. Kevin's just renting me out and watching. He doesn't fuck outside the basement."

"Sounds fun. Let me walk you to the station," Aled said. "S'only down the hill. C'mon."

Gabriel's hand was damp and warm in his own, and Aled figured there'd been two orgasms in the alley instead of one. Gabriel refused to agree, calling him imaginative as Aled tucked himself away and they stepped back out of the dark and into the gentle yellow glow pouring from the pub windows like nothing had ever happened, hand in hand.

"Hey!"

Gabriel stiffened, darting his hand away from Aled's in a flash. And Aled frowned. He knew that shout. He'd heard it once before.

"Oh, I don't fucking believe it," Gabriel whispered.

"I've had enough of this!"

Aled remembered a white-knuckled hand on a doorframe just before the car door slammed. Then he lost his temper.

"Jesus Christ, will you just *fuck off*!"

Gabriel jumped away from him like he'd been shot. Michael stopped in the middle of the road. Aled unbuttoned his lip and let the beer do the talking.

"Grow the fuck up and let go already! It's over! *Over*, need me to spell it out? O-V-E—"

"Like I'm going to let him just fuck off with an abusive scum—"

People were coming out of the pub. Tom was suddenly shouldering his way through to stand beside him. Gabriel was hovering on the curb, one foot in the road and one out of it.

Aled was short, ginger and had been wearing glasses since he was eight years old. He'd known men like Michael all his life. Men who thought a six-pack and a sizeable sausage made them God's gift to the known world. Men who had thinner skin than the loo roll in a public toilet. Men who thought that sex was just them getting to shove their dick somewhere and to hell with who accommodated it. Sex with them was enough, right? Sex with them was automatically brilliant because *they* were automatically brilliant. There'd always been men like Michael. There always *would* be men like Michael.

And yet here they were. With Michael staking out a pub like an obsessed loser and Aled having been the recipient of a birthday blowjob.

"Fuck me," he said. "What kind of sad cunt stalks their ex? What's the matter, Michael — was nobody else willing to go for a ride on your prick?"

Everything moved.

Michael first. Fist up, surging forward.

Then Tom, smashing between them like a shield.

Then Gabriel.

Who jumped off the curb like it was a trampoline and slammed his fist into Michael's perfect jaw with the loudest crack that Aled had ever heard.

Chapter Twenty

The cell door opened and Gabriel looked up from his examination of the floor.

"There's an interview room free, Mr Lazarri," said the cop. "Let's grab our chance, eh?"

He was middle-aged, with little round glasses and a bald spot, and a soft voice that reminded Gabriel of nurses. He looked more like a geography teacher than a copper, and Gabriel appreciated it. The ones that had broken up the fight outside the pub last night had been rough and aggressive, but the custody staff were all right. And it wasn't exactly Gabriel's first time being arrested either. The food was as shit as ever, but the mattress was surprisingly comfortable and Gabriel had managed a few hours before someone had been dragged in at five in the morning, screaming the place down and calling them all fascist scum. And it looked like the morning shift were friendlier than their late-night counterparts, because the officer held out a cup of coffee and apologised for it being instant.

"It'll do," Gabriel said.

"Come with me, then. Let's not keep you waiting too much longer, eh?"

Gabriel had been arrested once or twice when he'd been begging, but that had been a long time ago and he couldn't really remember what came after a kip in the cells. He fidgeted as the officer set up a tape and got his notebook out. His colleague was already nodding off. Gabriel sympathised.

"All right, interview commencing at nine-thirteen. Interviewing officer is myself, PC 6453 David Barnes, and I am accompanied by my colleague, PC 4521 Peter Rice. If you can just say your name for the tape, please, sir."

"Gabriel James Lazarri."

"Thank you."

They went through his rights and Gabriel shrugged off the offer of a lawyer. It was just a punch-up, and he hadn't been arrested in years. Why bother with a lawyer for a stupid punch-up? Going by the dozing PC Rice, they weren't even going to bother getting him in front of a magistrate for a telling off and a fine. He was probably going to just get cautioned again.

"Could you tell me in your own words what happened, Mr Lazarri?"

Gabriel opened his mouth—and paused.

He'd been ready to say it was just a dumb fight. He'd been ready to say he lost his temper, it all got a bit out of hand, things happen, he hoped the other guy was all right, whoever he was, never seen him before. He'd been ready to blow it off as one drink too many, keep quiet that he'd been sober as a priest, and nothing more.

But his wrist throbbed in memory of Michael's grab outside work.

His phone was full of messages.

Kevin.

Aled.

"It was my partner's thirty-fifth birthday. He'd gone out with friends earlier in the day, and I'd been busy, so I went to meet him at the pub once I was done with my other stuff. I didn't want to go inside, because I'm a recovering alcoholic, so I asked him to come out. When he did, my ex turned up and they started shouting at each other. My ex has been harassing us for weeks and went to hit my partner, so I stepped in to defend him. Then my ex hit me back, so my partner and his friend waded in, and the police turned up."

He and Michael had been arrested. Tom had managed to keep Aled out of it and Gabriel owed him big time for that one.

"What's your partner's name?"

"Aled Evans."

"Do you know which friend of his got involved?"

"I do, but I'd rather not say," Gabriel replied cautiously.

"And your ex-partner?"

"Michael. I don't know his last name. It was just a casual thing to me. I know his address, though."

"Please."

He furnished them with all the addresses — his old flat, Michael's terraced house, Aled's little nook — and the number plate of Michael's car. It had been personalised. Of course Michael was the type to get a personalised number plate on a ten-year-old Clio.

"And you say Michael has been harassing you?"

"Yeah. We broke up last month."

"Could you be more specific about the harassment?"

Gabriel took a deep breath. Here it went. All or nothing.

He'd never really been pro-police before the PCSO who'd got him off the streets in Sheffield. They had always been the dark figures in the night who came to lock up his mum and her partner of the week when they'd been fighting. A threat if he misbehaved. A danger lurking on the way to school, shadowed faces under shadowed hats. Something to be avoided and mistrusted — first because he was from Hackney then because he was homeless then because he was queer. When that PCSO had first stopped by Gabriel's pitch, the first question out of Gabriel's mouth had been, *'What do you care?'*

It had taken years to shake the idea that maybe they weren't the devil in black and yellow, and were really just like anyone else he'd ever met — but it still took a moment for him to unlock his jaw and tell the story he should have been telling them from the start.

He told them about the text messages.

He told them about the argument on the landing.

He told them about Kevin's story — although he left out Kevin offering to sort it.

He told them about the car following them back to the motorway.

He told them about the scene outside the shop.

And he told them that the car had been waiting, yet again, for him and Aled to come out of the pub.

Then he sat back, pushed his instant coffee away and said, "Actually, can I have that lawyer, please? I want to talk about getting a restraining order."

* * * *

It was raining when he stepped out of the police station, and Aled's car was waiting across the road.

Gabriel jogged through the puddles but was dripping wet by the time he slid into the front passenger seat and laughed when he was immediately offered a towel.

"Kevin called," Aled said. "You might have some angry voicemail messages."

"What did you tell him?"

"The truth," Aled replied. "He was pissed at you for getting yourself in the way of a fight, but—he understands, too."

"Great," Gabriel said. "So I'm not going to get beaten, but Michael's flat is on fire. How long have you been here?"

"About an hour," Aled said, turning the heater up. "Are you all right?"

"Fine. It's not the first time."

"I don't wanna—"

"I told them about Michael stalking me."

Aled cut himself off mid-word and stared.

"I'm done," Gabriel said, folding up the damp towel and setting it down in the footwell. "I deserved better than him from the start. I have better than him and I have it in spades. I'm going to get another job and get back into cycling. I haven't been out on the bike since this whole mess started. I'm going to find a club or something. And I'm going to get a restraining order so if Michael comes sniffing around again, I can have him arrested. I'm done. Last night was the final straw."

"Sorry," Aled said. "Still a bit slow. Blame the hangover. Or shock. You've—filed a complaint?"

"I reported a crime."

"To the *police*?"

"Yeah."

"And—"

"And they have to look into it. They're going to give it to someone from their domestic abuse team. I showed them all my messages. And they're going to ring you and Kevin and ask about it. Do you keep your dashcam footage?"

"Er, yeah, for a few days…"

"Do you have it still from when he followed us away from the flat?"

"Probably."

"You can send them that, then. And—"

Aled held up both hands. "Hold up. Can I get a recording of this? The guy who was blasé about being used like a sex toy and never getting an orgasm from some steroid-guzzling airhead has finally admitted he deserves better?"

"Well, I at least deserve the orgasms," Gabriel quipped.

Aled laughed. It was his surprised wheeze, as if it had been punched out of him, and secretly it was Gabriel's favourite laugh. He curled his toes in his shoes and grinned at the windscreen until Aled had recovered.

"You deserve the world," Aled said, and Gabriel whined at him for being cheesy. "Shut up, it's true. I'm glad you've seen sense about him at any rate."

Gabriel shrugged, heat rising in his face.

"So I'm slow. Big deal."

"Hey, no slower than me. I even felt a bit sorry for him at the start."

"You what?"

Aled pulled a face. "I know what it's like, remember? To have someone you're enthralled by walk away from you. I know what it's like to watch someone incredible slip through your fingers. The way I acted with Melissa, trying to deny her the divorce — that wasn't acceptable either."

"You didn't stalk her or deck her new boyfriend."

"I wanted to."

"But you didn't."

Aled shrugged. "I got where he was coming from is what I'm saying. It wasn't okay, but — yeah. I could understand him on an emotional level. At first. And it's a little scary to look at him, to be honest, because I could easily have gone that way with Melissa."

"Uh-huh," Gabriel said. "But you didn't. And the reason he lost me is because of how he treated me in the first place, because if he'd been decent to me, you wouldn't have minded him and none of this would have happened."

Aled nodded.

Gabriel licked his lips and took a deep breath before continuing. "Thank you."

"For what?"

"For challenging things without trying to change me."

Slowly, Aled wound his fingers around Gabriel's.

"You were uncomfortable because of how he treated me. You're fine with Kevin — you get along with Kevin, even. But Michael made you feel antsy, and it was because of how he treated me. And I didn't really see how he treated me until you were pointing it out. So…thanks. I've got room for better people now. And I'm going to find some."

It was just Aled and Kevin now. And that was too weighted in one direction. Gabriel needed the hotel room flings and loud gigs. Someone to go cycling with, maybe. Or camping — proper wild camping, not Aled's cabin-in-the-woods pussying-out version. Maybe he could get another boyfriend, too. Proper dates and stuff, when Aled was working and Kevin was too married-with-kids for midnight screenings of the latest blockbuster and Nando's on a Saturday afternoon.

"Can you postpone the finding someone until tomorrow?" Aled asked.

Gabriel raised his eyebrows. "Maybe. Why?"

The hand holding his own tightened.

"I want to play a game."

Gabriel licked his lips, casually shifting in the seat to open his knees a fraction.

"What kind of a game?"

"You caused a fight. I think you ought to pay for my black eye, don't you?"

The hand migrated to his thigh and squeezed. Gabriel grinned and squirmed before dropping his gaze and adopted a more contrite air.

"I'm sorry, sir."

Green.

"You will be."

Aled started the engine and, as they peeled out into traffic, Gabriel risked a peek in the wing mirror. No familiar car following. No Michael in their wake. Nothing.

Just him and Aled—and, by the tone, a pair of handcuffs and the radiator in the spare room.

Perfect.

E p i l o g u e

There was a letter on the mat when Aled came downstairs.

He didn't tend to get much post, and the blue crest caught his eye. Police. It was addressed to both of them, but *really* it was meant for Gabriel.

Aled hesitated then tore into it anyway.

Victim care. A fairly standard boilerplate bracketing the details. And Aled's tension eased. The restraining order — covering the whole of Wakefield — had been granted. Three months arguing with lawyers had paid off — and paid off well. The area was bigger than they'd hoped for and it had been granted for a year. That was more than enough to shake him off.

Especially if Gabriel agreed to —

Aled took a deep breath and propped the letter up on the side. They could discuss what to do about it later. Michael had a year to cool his heels and get over being dumped. They had a year to sort something out. And sorting something out would be so much easier if Gabriel agreed to stay.

But Aled wasn't going to think about any of it right now Gabriel was due out of his job interview any minute, and Aled had designs on whisking him off for a pub lunch somewhere in the country, with convenient lay-bys for a lay on the way home if Gabriel were amenable to a quick and dirty fumble somewhere. If the interview had gone well, perhaps a slow and sensual lay at home instead. If it had gone badly, a commiseration screw in a public toilet, perhaps. It was the middle of March, but the weather felt more like the middle of June. If it had gone *really* badly, maybe even a fuck in some cold mud somewhere and a game to go with it. That would cheer Gabriel up.

Although...

Aled would never admit it, but he was hoping it had gone badly. He felt bad for even feeling it and would never breathe a word of it to Gabriel, but the longer it took Gabriel to find another job, the longer he'd have to stay. And Aled wanted him to stay. Permanently.

He'd not say a word, though. Not until the time came for Gabriel to make the decision.

And anyway, if Gabriel *did* go, well, Aled would just have to up the ante, wouldn't he? And persuade him to come back. Permanently.

Pushing the question aside, Aled locked up behind him as his phone buzzed. He ignored it, knowing it would just be his summons to come and collect His Majesty, and drove with the windows down and the radio on loud. His foot was slightly too heavy on the accelerator and he let himself enjoy it. He couldn't influence Gabriel's decision either way and it could be ages before he found another job anyway. So why worry? Pick him up, spoil him rotten, undress just enough to play with and bring them both to a high. He wouldn't need long to do it either — Gabriel had left at eight for this interview, without so much as a goodbye kiss. Bastard.

The interview was at Aled's gym and he almost autopiloted his way to the spaces by the trees before rolling his eyes and swerving around to the entrance. Gabriel was standing by the bike racks, texting furiously, and Aled rolled right up in front of him.

"Oi! You," he said. Gabriel jumped. "Face. Here. Now."

Gabriel laughed, his whole face lighting up. Then, rather than lean in through the window, he opened the driver's door and crashed into Aled's mouth and chest, the kiss hungry and lopsided, the hug too hot and awkward.

"I got it!"

"Sorry?" Aled asked, a little dazed.

"I got it! I got the job!"

So much for time.

Gabriel didn't seem to notice Aled's stunned silence, near-bouncing around the car to jump into the passenger seat and enthusing a mile a minute about the interviewer, the team members, the shift pattern, the free use of the facilities…

"I mean, the pay's not great and it's only part-time, but it's a start and —"

"Celebratory drink?"

"Pitstop on the way? I'm *buzzing*! I need —" A hand strayed to Aled's thigh. "Something, you know, to take the edge off…"

Aled's stomach churned. He wanted to beam and enthuse. Wanted to run them out through Brandy Carr and a lonely field. Wanted to buy lunch and tease about perhaps coming for a swim when Gabriel was at work and taking him in the changing rooms while his colleagues mopped floors two feet away...

But all he could think was about home.

About coming home to an empty house again. About having space in the wardrobes. About having to arrange dates and visits. About no more foot massages in the middle of the news, random kisses at the sink or waking up when he was smacked to let Gabriel go for his three-in-the-morning piss.

About taking several steps backwards, when all he wanted to do was go forward.

"Aled?"

"Sorry?"

"Is everything okay?"

"Yeah, yeah, sorry, just distracted."

Out of the corner of his eye, he saw Gabriel bite his lip.

"You don't seem happy about this."

Aled exhaled heavily then decided to hell with it. He pulled over, ignoring the driver who hit his horn behind them, and hauled on the handbrake.

"Okay," he said. "There is no way of saying this that isn't going to make you wary, especially after everything that's happened, but the simple fact is, I don't want you to go."

"What?"

"You moved in because you lost your job. And now you have a new one. And it's always your choice — it's absolutely your choice — I'd never try to *stop* you, but — I don't want you to move out again. I want — I want evenings in with the telly, I want your bitching about the state of my kitchen, I want your feet to end up in my lap like you're owed a foot massage just for bloody well existing, I want — "

"Yes."

Aled's heart hiccupped.

"What?"

"I want that too. I want to stay."

The hiccup turned into a shiver.

"You—really?"

"Yeah."

"I don't have to bring out the big bribery guns?"

"A foot massage a day kind of counts, right?"

Aled laughed. It sounded reed-thin and shaky. "You're seriously agreeing to stay moved in with me?"

Gabriel flushed lightly and nodded. "Yes. I mean…Jesus, Aled, I think I've figured out you're not going to turn into what I was afraid of. And I love you. So…yeah. I want to stay. If you'd let me."

"Let you? You kidding me? Seriously, Gabe, last chance of backing out, 'cause after one more yes, I won't let you go without a hell of a fight. Divorce-level fight. Sure?"

Gabriel laughed.

And all he said was, "*Gabriel.*"

Aled surged across the car and kissed him.

It wasn't romantic. It wasn't sweet. It wasn't even dirty—it was a harsh clash of lips and teeth, painful and too sudden and smeared sideways by Gabriel's laughter. It was messy, clutching hands and traffic roaring past them and the heat too oppressive to be tolerated.

"Fuck the pub," Aled said hoarsely. "When's your first shift?"

"At the gym?"

"Yeah."

"Why?"

"Need to know how rough I can be," Aled said, grinning and palming Gabriel's thigh. "Home. Our home. You and me. Our—hall floor. I'm not getting further than that. I'm going to christen the hall floor with you *then* I'll take you out to lunch."

Gabriel wound both hands into Aled's hair and kissed him.

"Hall floor," he breathed. "Order takeaway. Then we can work on the living room carpet."

Want to see more from this author?
Here's a taster for you to enjoy!

Enough
Matthew J. Metzger

Excerpt

He could smell the fire.

He was blind. His eyes streamed. The curling wallpaper crackled and hissed. His skin was burning. The air in his lungs seared him from the inside out. And there was nowhere to go—no escape from the heat, no escape from the orange towers and acrid black smoke, no *air*.

"Ezra!"

The smoke wrapped itself around his teeth and tongue like a grotesque mockery of a kiss, and there was no reply but the roar of hot air and climbing fire. The house was burning. *The house was burning!*

"Ezra! Ez!"

A scream. A piercing scream, like nothing he'd ever heard, but before he could move, the wooden boards crumbled to ash and he was falling, tearing through the shreds of stairs into the inferno, and—

Jesse hit the carpet with a thump and jarred himself awake.

The flat was quiet. The streetlight touched the other side of the curtains with a faint orange light. There was no smoke, no fire, no sound. Nothing.

Jesse dragged himself back onto the bed. The sheets were impossibly tangled and his tank top stuck to him with sweat. His wrist ached in its brace where he'd bumped it, but the panic hadn't quite eased its grip on his heart or his lungs, and he fumbled for his phone, ignoring the pain.

Thank God for speed dial.

The clock on the side said two-fifty-eight, and the phone rang six times before the line coughed and crackled and a sleepy voice, tinged in the early hours with the fading edges of a Welsh accent, mumbled a vague sort of question.

"Ez?"

There was a rustle of sheets. "Jesse?"

"Oh, God," Jesse breathed. The air escaped in a rush, loud and hard. His lungs shook with the effort. "Shit. I just— I needed to check—"

"Jess? What's happened, sweetheart?"

The soft roll of his vowels, the accent entirely muted when he was properly awake, was as comforting as a hug, and Jesse coughed out, "Nightmare," before thinking twice. Ezra was okay. He was okay. It was all okay.

"Oh, sweetheart," Ezra murmured, low and crooning. "Do you want to tell me about it?"

"I need—can I come over? I know it's late and I know you have work in the morning, but—I just—I need—"

"No," Ezra interrupted, and Jesse's stomach twisted violently.

"*Please*, Ez, I—"

"Hey, hey, hey." Ezra cut him off. "Hey, stop, calm down, sweetheart. I *meant* you can't come here. You don't sound okay, not to me, and I don't want you to go out like this, so I'll come to you, all right?"

Jesse exhaled, the twist easing. "Okay."

"You okay if I hang up, or do you want me to put the phone on speaker?"

"Can — speaker," Jesse swallowed against the nausea. He was still shaking, he realised faintly. "I just — I couldn't find you, Ez. The house was burning and I couldn't find you, and I — I need to hear you. You don't have to talk to me, but I need to hear you."

"Okay." The phone crackled again and clunked, and suddenly Ezra's voice was loud and echoing. Soothing. The Welsh hint was fading, and Jesse could suddenly hear him dressing, but he was *there*. "Was it my house or the one last week?"

"Yours," Jesse said. "I was on the stairs, and they gave way, and I woke up. I couldn't find you."

"If my house was on fire, I would probably be in the kitchen having caused it," Ezra said, and yawned loudly. "Make yourself useful, sweetheart, and make up a brew for me? I've not slept long."

Jesse knew better than to apologise. He shrugged out of his sweat-soaked pyjamas and pulled on a pair of jogging bottoms before taking the phone through the narrow hall into the kitchen. The kitchen window overlooked the main road. A police car trailed idly by on the prowl. Phone to his ear, he listened to Ezra swear sleepily at his cupboard, and the soft sounds of those narrow feet padding downstairs.

"Sweetheart?"

"Mm?" Jesse listened to the front door and the heavy sound of the key.

"I'm going to hang up while I drive. You all right for ten minutes until I get there?"

"Yeah," Jesse croaked. His heart had come down out of the rafters, and he could breathe. The streetlights didn't look threatening anymore. He just felt…shaky. Sick and shaky and scared. "Yeah, Ez, I'll be fine."

"Okay. Love you."

The dial tone was immediate. Jesse dropped the phone to the counter and switched on the kettle, staring out of the window and waiting, arms folded against the chill. It wasn't the first nightmare, and it wouldn't be the last. He usually managed one a week without fail, and the injury hadn't helped matters. But they didn't usually involve Ezra in burning buildings. They didn't usually involve losing him.

And Jesse couldn't stomach the thought of losing him.

Which was a bit scary in itself. They'd only met eight months ago. At a gay bar, of all places—the one place where he went to meet sex partners, not partner partners. Jesse had thought the freckled blond with the dark eyes was pretty in the neon lights and had bought him a drink, talked him into a dance, bought him another. Kissed him at the back of the dance floor—and had promptly found himself alone, but with a phone number in his back pocket.

He'd wanted sex. That was all he'd been after. Sex with a pretty guy. But then they'd gone on a date and he'd met Ezra properly, and he was lost. Ezra wasn't just a handsome face and nice legs. Ezra was the world. He was Jesse's world, and it had only been eight months, but Jesse still knew that this was it, for him. Ezra was it. There would never be anyone else like him.

So he stood in a tense vigil at the window, waiting for the faithful little Peugeot 207 to creep around the corner. Waiting for Ezra to come, because there was emotional shock and there was sense, and the two weren't in line right now. He knew Ezra was okay. He knew it. He'd answered the phone. He'd been sleepy and understanding and sworn at his cupboard. He was fine.

But Jesse still needed to reach out and touch him, just to make sure. *Somehow.*

The little blue car was lonely on the three-in-the-morning road, and Jesse propped the door of his flat to creep down the communal stairs and open the main door. Ezra had gotten sort-of dressed, in jeans and an open check shirt, feet shoved into his trainers without socks, and his hair was wild and fluffy, in gleeful disarray, as he locked the car and wrapped himself around Jesse in a tight, warm hug.

Jesse clung back until something creaked, and pressed the side of his face against that wild hair.

"You're all right, sweetheart," Ezra murmured.

Jesse squeezed again until Ezra's grip on the nape of his neck tightened in warning, then he let go and dragged Ezra up the silent stairs by the hand. Concrete stairs. They wouldn't collapse in a fire until the whole building came down.

He didn't say a word until he'd pressed the requested tea into Ezra's hands, locked the door again and bundled them both back to the messy bed. Ezra was equally silent, taking a couple of mouthfuls before abandoning the tea, stripping to his underwear and crawling into the mess to mould himself into Jesse's arms.

"There you go," he murmured lowly, kissing Jesse's encroaching stubble and stroking a hand gently through his hair. "Feel better now?"

"Mm," Jesse pressed his nose into Ezra's neck, tangling their legs together. He could feel a strong pulse in Ezra's jugular. He could feel the rough skin of the bumpy scar on Ezra's shoulder under his fingertips. He could feel the fuzzy mess of Ezra's hair, usually styled and stiff in that messy-but-it's-on-purpose-so-it's-okay manner, now just loose and wild. He could feel *him*. "Thank you."

"Thank me again tomorrow afternoon when I'm grumpy and exhausted after two hours of the Year Nines."

"Okay," Jesse agreed, sliding his arms completely around Ezra's back until he enveloped him. They didn't often sleep cuddled together—or even together at all, between Ezra's eight-to-four and Jesse's shifts—but he needed this. He *needed* it.

"Mind if I go to sleep?"

"No," Jesse squirmed until Ezra got the hint and tucked his head under his chin. His hair tickled. Jesse kissed the top of his head and wished he had the easy grace with language that Ezra did. Wished he could express himself properly. Wished he could talk as easily as he hugged. But all that came out was, "I just needed to touch you."

Ezra said nothing to that, simply shifting until he was comfortable, one arm over Jesse's ribs and the other tucked over his own waist in a casual sort of drop. Ezra was *long*—long limbs, long neck, all willowy lines and bendy joints, and he settled like water into the bulkier, stiffer contours of Jesse's body.

But he fit, and he fit perfectly, and Jesse wrapped him up and held him, breathing in the smell of store-brand shampoo and cheap aftershave until the last traces of the nightmare-induced fear washed away.

It was still a long time before he slept.

PUBLISHING

Sign up for our newsletter and find out about all our romance book releases, eBook sales and promotions, sneak peeks and FREE romance books!

About the Author

Matthew J. Metzger is an asexual, transgender British author juggling books, an office job and a love of travel with the human need for sleep once in a while. He writes both adult and young adult books focusing on LGBT+ characters and their relationships, particularly those from the less salubrious areas in which he was dragged up over the years.

On the very rare occasions that Matt isn't writing, he can usually be found at the gym, halfway up a mountain or collecting new tattoos. (And yes, he does have book ink...)

Matthew loves to hear from readers. You can find his contact information, website details and author profile page at https://www.pride-publishing.com